danger.com

@1//Gemini7/

First Aladdin Paperbacks edition October 1997

Copyright © 1997 by Jordan Cray

Aladdin Paperbacks
An imprint of Simon & Schuster
Children's Publishing Division
1230 Avenue of the Americas
New York, NY 10020

The text of this book was set in 10.5-Sabon

Printed and bound in the United States of America

10 9 8 7 6 5 4

Library of Congress Cataloging-in-Publication Data
Cray, Jordan.
Gemini7 / Jordan Cray. -- 1st Aladdin Paperbacks ed.
p. cm. -- (danger.com)
Summary: When the dream girl he meets on the Internet
shows up as a real person, Jonah watches his totally
exciting other life turn into a nightmare.
ISBN 0-689-81432-1
[1. Interpersonal relations--Fiction. 2. Internet (Computer net-
works)--Fiction. 3. Computers--Fiction.] I. Title. II. Series.
PZ7.C85315Gh   1997
[Fic]--dc21   97-5112
CIP   AC

danger.com

@1//Gemini7/

by
jordan.cray

Aladdin Paperbacks

//prologue

First, you have your outside self. The self who eats breakfast, talks to people, gets her teeth cleaned once a year.

Second, you have the other you. The real one. The one who wakes up in the middle of the night in a panic. The one who feels like she is on the other side of a mirror, watching everybody else. The one who stares at something like her little finger, or her reflection in a window, and wonders, what makes this finger, this face mine? What attaches me to this cage of flesh and bones?

That's when I panic. All I want to do is run as long and as hard as I can until I collapse and am too tired to think for one more second, because if I do, I'll start screaming and won't be able to stop.

That's what she thought about.

Every day, she worried about the two selves that were hers. But even in her panic, she also believed in answers. There was an answer for everything, if you thought about it long enough. And that meant there was a solution, if you planned hard enough. She wasn't a straight-A student just because of a lame school system. She was smart, and she knew a secret: Most kids only study school subjects. That's where they went wrong. Life is a subject in itself. You have to study hard for it, just like school.

Nobody ever knows what people really think about. You present a face to the world, and the world accepts that face, and even if people say stupid things like, "How do you feel about that?" or, "Penny for your thoughts," they don't really want to know.

So if you looked at TV, and magazines, and movies, and if you went to the grocery store, or even sat by the lake and watched the swans, and you *studied* what you saw, you knew that the answer was a number.

Two.

If there was nothing between you and empty space, you were lost. But if there was one person who loved you more than anything, you had something between you and the darkness. One person in your corner. One person to defend you. To keep you safe. Forever.

Looking at him was like looking in a mirror.

Every time you gazed into his eyes, you saw yourself.

Suddenly, having two selves didn't matter when you were with him. And that made you whole.

That's the best feeling in the world, she thought. *And it's worth sacrificing anything I have to do to keep it.*

Anything.

you've got mail!

To:whoever@cyberspace.com
From:JonBoy
Subject:babes in space

Most guys think I'm lucky. I have a girl-friend. Jen and I have been going steady since junior high. I made a joke in the cafeteria, and she laughed so hard that soda came out of her nose. Right then, I knew she was the girl for me.

So I'd snagged my girlfriend early. Back when Jenny Malone was still skinny as a flag-pole and had a long braid down her back tied with a droopy plaid ribbon. Back when peanut butter got stuck in her braces, and she raised her hand in class to answer every question. In short, Jenny Malone was well in sight of geek territory.

Now, at sixteen, you could say that Jen has improved. Okay, maybe they wouldn't ask her to do a slo-mo run on the beach in Ocean

Avenue, *my favorite TV show*. But now her teeth are straight, and her feathery hair is the color of an autumn leaf. Her hazel eyes are surrounded by thick black lashes that she likes to flutter at me to make me laugh. And she has one terrific zillion-megawatt smile.

So who's complaining?

Moi.

I live in a small town. Milleridge, Pennsylvania, to be exact. Every single pretty girl within a thirty-mile radius thinks of me as Jenny Malone's personal property. I can barely smile *at* a girl without it getting around school in about five minutes flat that I'm a major slimeball weevil.

Okay. Here's my point. I totally crave tuna melts. But I wouldn't want to eat one for lunch every single day. Sometimes you just want turkey. Or heck, even Spam.

But around Milleridge High, Jonah-and-Jen is practically one word.

"Are JonahandJen coming to the party?"

"Did JonahandJen see Mayhem, Part Four?"

Or, worst of all, no matter where I show up, from the park to the river to the mall, I hear:

"Hey, Jonah. Where's Jen?"

After a while, you start to wonder if just being *you* is enough.

Then one day, I took a ride with the top down, cruise control engaged, on the information superhighway. On the Net, I can smile at whoever I want. Of course, it looks like this:

:-)

But it's better than no action at all.

Pretty soon I had six girlfriends. And I developed deep, meaningful relationships with each one of them. It was real, but it wasn't. I still had Jen. I still had my real life. But alongside of it was this totally exciting other life, where I could flirt with all sorts of different girls.

It wasn't really real. At least that's what I told myself. I wasn't hurting Jen.

The only problem was, sometimes doing something you think is sorta wrong and kinda sneaky but basically harmless . . . well, it doesn't mean that there won't be a price to pay.

And it can be way higher than you'd ever imagined.

1//same old same old

In my humble opinion—or IMHO, in cyber talk—whoever invented school totally goofed. Final exams should be in February, or even March—sometime during those gray, freezing days when it hurts to breathe because the air is so cold and you're positive it's going to be winter forever. Having finals in February would be a package deal marked Everything Sucks.

But take June. What kind of a human being, especially a *kid* human, wants to sit hunched over his books when it's just getting warm enough to swim? Who can keep his concentration on formulas and numbers when summer is right in his face, breathing warm air and green grass and blue sky?

If you want my opinion, they're just asking kids to flunk out.

I wasn't close to flunking—not for nothing do I have a straight-A girlfriend. But when it came to trig, I was hanging on by my fingernails to that C-minus cliff, in great danger of dropping into the burning D river. Jen had promised to help me study, but I always found an excuse not to. Like, I had to wash my dad's car. Or play dolls with my little sister, Annie. Can you tell I'd rather do anything but trig?

One particular stellar day Jen had scheduled another study session after school. The final bell rang, and I headed for my locker. After I got my jacket and books, I'd meet Jen at her locker. We'd walk home together. Jen lives right next door, and we'd sit in her family room, or on the back porch if it was warm out, and pretend to study while we ate cookies or leftover pizza. Then we'd shoot some hoops, or watch MTV, or listen to a new CD, and then I'd go home for dinner. After dinner, I'd call her about eight o'clock, and we'd talk some more. Jen would say, "Well, homework calls, Jones, gotta split," after about twenty minutes. Then I'd say, "Pick you up outside tomorrow," and she'd say, "If you're lucky," and we'd hang up.

How did I know this would happen, just like that?

Because it happened every day, just like that.

At my locker, I reached for my denim jacket and my trig book. I slammed the door shut and twirled the lock. My trig book fell on the ground, and I kicked it.

"Young man! Young man!" My best friend, Matt Staple, wagged a finger in my face. He pitched his voice high and shaky. "Treat your things well, and they'll return the favor." Matt was doing his impersonation of Miss Levering, our horrible teacher from back in fourth grade. You might say that Matt and I have some history together.

I picked up my trig book and stuffed it in my backpack. "Die laughing, Mr. Comedian."

I meant it to come out funny, but my tone was like curdled milk. Matt took a step back. "Hey, what's up with you?"

I sighed as I put on my jacket. I knew that it wasn't fair to take my cranky mood out on Matt. Let alone my trig book. "Finals pressure is getting to me, man," I said. I gripped my hair with both hands and widened my eyes. "I think I'm going to crack like an egg! Help me! Help me! *Aaarrggg!*"

Matt pretended not to notice my bonehead activity. "So where's Jen?" he asked, twirling his lock.

"*Arrrrgggg!*" I said again, banging my head against a locker.

"What are you guys up to?" Matt asked as he stuffed some books in his knapsack.

I was getting a headache from banging my head, so I gave up acting like an idiot. "Same old same old," I said. "You?"

"Study date with Alison Potasher," Matt said. He shook his hand, as though his fingers were burning. "*Va-va-va-voom-de-ay.*"

"How did you get a date with Alison Potasher, nerdling?" I asked. Alison is major dream girl material. She can run in slow motion on my beach anytime.

Matt grinned as he slammed his locker shut. "I'm pulling A's in social studies *and* trig," he said. "This time of year, I can have my pick. All I have to do is say the word 'tutor,' and babes come running."

"Whoa," I said. "I never thought being a coma-inducing grind could actually improve your date potential. Radical thinking."

Matt shrugged modestly. "My own personal strategy. Tomorrow, Emily Beringer and I have a social studies date."

"Wow," I said. "I totally salute you, dude."

"Oh, tutor!" Alison Potasher waggled her fingers at Matt from down the hall. Her green eyes sparkled as she tossed her coppery red hair flirtatiously. "Are you ready to rock and roll?"

"I'm there!" Matt called back.

Alison pursed her lips and frowned. Can I

just say this? It's amazing how girls can project pouts, all the way down a crowded hallway.

"Just be gentle with me, Matt," she cooed. The girl is so good, she can project a coo.

"What can I say," Matt said to me under his breath while he grinned like a monkey at Alison. "I looooove finals week."

I watched Matt join Alison at her locker. I wondered if Alison's cinnamon-colored hair would smell a little spicy if you got up real close.

I speeded up the pace toward Jen's locker. I was about two minutes and forty-five seconds late. What can I say? You get your excitement in life where you can.

2//togetherforever

Jen greeted me with such a big smile that I felt guilty about wondering what Alison's hair would smell like.

"Hey, Jones," Jen said, pulling out her sweater. "Ready for some hard-core trig drill?"

"Oh, did you say we were going to do *trig drill*?" I said. "I thought you said we were going to fire up the *big grill*. I was looking forward to a couple of hot dogs."

Jen grinned as she closed her locker. "Relax, Jonah. It's as easy as falling off a logarithm."

"Another comedian. Is this actually clown school?" I said. "Funny, because I thought I was in Milleridge High."

Jen slipped her arm through mine. "C'mon, Oscar the Grouch. I've got a brownie with your name on it. No walnuts."

Hey, there's an advantage to having a steady girl. She knows what you're allergic to.

We headed out of school together. We said

"see you" to all our friends together. Started home together.

Our legs moved together. Our feet hit the ground together. Our pace seemed to stamp the word into my brain.

Together . . . together . . . *together.*

Jen and I both live in big old houses near the center of town. Most kids live in the newer developments outside Milleridge. The town was settled along the banks of the Delaware River sometime before the Revolutionary War. My family's house was built in 1798. In the winter, I swear I can feel each and every crack in the old walls from the wind whistling through them. A few years ago, before Dad replaced the furnace, I found ice on my toothbrush one morning. People always say how *charming* our house is. Try living with icicles in your blood every winter. You call that charm?

But at least Mom and Dad keep up with repairs on our old shack. They are totally mad about renovation projects. Jen's house is falling down around her ears. Her dad never was much of a handyman in the first place. Her mom used to rag him about it, especially when she saw my dad fixing the plumbing and painting the shutters.

But maybe Jen's mom shouldn't have said a

word. Mr. Malone started hanging around Bob's Hardware Station every Saturday. He got really interested in drill bits and two-by-fours. And then the summer before last he ran away with Trudie Belden, the twenty-two-year-old cashier.

The funny thing was, Jen didn't talk about it. And the girl was never shy before about letting you know what was on her mind. But whenever I asked her about her dad leaving, she just got this really intense look on her face and said that everything was going to be okay. Her dad hadn't been such a swell guy when he was around. He had spent all his time in his "office" in the basement, where Jen said all he did was watch TV and read magazines. But I had a feeling that no matter what kind of a dad you had, no matter if he never came to one of your swim meets or softball games, you still had to miss him when he left.

But Jen was okay with it. Or as okay as she could be. Her older brother, Scott, had been the one to go off the deep end. He'd flunked out of college and taken a job in a restaurant in New Jersey. Then he'd gotten into some pretty heavy drugs, and Mrs. Malone had been really worried about him for a while. Jen's dad lived about three towns upriver, and even he'd gotten involved, maybe for the first time since he'd had kids. He'd paid for a therapist over in Doylestown, and had even bought Scott a used car so he could drive there.

Now Scott has straightened out and is going to Penn State. So the Malones are doing all right. If their house doesn't collapse on their heads, that is.

Jen drilled me on trig for a while, but my mind was wandering. Even the sugar rush from the brownie didn't help my concentration.

"Jonah, I know this is Dullsville, but you've got to work on it," Jen said, tapping my leg with her pencil. "If you pull a D, your parents will flip. And you'll probably have to go to summer school, which would be a major drag. It might interfere with your job. Not to mention my summer," she teased.

Oh, did I mention that Jen and I had jobs at the country club? *Together?* I would be bussing tables at the club restaurant, and she was on the grounds crew.

I'd get to see Jen every day. We'd drive there together, and eat lunch together, and drive home together. I could see the whole summer stretching ahead of me. I knew what I'd be doing every day and every evening. . . .

Together. Together. *Together . . .*

Meanwhile, all around me, I'd see girls. Girls in shorts. Girls in bathing suits. Girls with long blond hair, girls with curly dark hair, girls with great legs, girls with great smiles, girls who flirted, girls who were shy.

And I wouldn't be able to talk to any of them.

Unless I broke up with Jen. But I didn't want to do that! I was crazy about her. Besides, every single person in Milleridge, including all the Malones and all of my family, the Laniers, *plus* Mr. Grandy at the ice-cream shop, would think I was a class-A slime weevil. Probably because I would *be* a class-A slime weevil if I dumped a girl like Jen.

Was there such a thing as being trapped into goodness?

"Jonah?" Jen peered at me. I knew the five freckles on her nose by heart. "What's wrong? You were staring at me like you wanted to strangle me. I just said you had to study harder, that's all."

I closed my book with a snap. "I know, you keep telling me. Every day at lunch. Every night on the phone. Every morning when we walk to school. Every—"

"Hey," Jen interrupted. "I'm just trying to help."

I didn't say anything, and Jen bent her head over her notebook. Her hair fell forward, so I couldn't see her face.

I looked at the Swatch Jen had bought me for my sixteenth birthday in October. It was almost four o'clock. I usually didn't leave for another hour, but I was anxious to get home. My girls were waiting. And today was a special day. I was expecting something important.

I had seven girlfriends on line. Amber, Katie, Marianne, Wendy, Patti, Jessica, and Nicole. I'd met them all in chat rooms, and we sent each other e-mail, too. Jessica lives in Hawaii, and she's totally cool to talk to. Amber is really smart and funny, and she lives only one state away in Ohio. She had been my favorite girlfriend. Until Nicole.

There was something special about Nicole, right from the start. We clicked in a major way. After we met on a chat line, we started going into private chat rooms so that we could talk without being interrupted. We'd been conversing for weeks now, and Nicole was the coolest ever. Today, she was sending me a picture of herself. I couldn't wait to download it.

Not that I was expecting a complete babe to pop up on my screen. Life isn't fair. I knew that. There was no way that Nicole could look as perfect as her personality was. But not *expecting* something great doesn't mean you can't *hope* for something great.

"You haven't asked me about my essay," Jen said, catching me zoning out the window.

"Oh. Sorry. How's your essay?" I asked.

"Thanks for asking," Jen said. She flashed me a grin, so I knew we were okay. "I worked on it again last night. Do you want to hear it?"

Jen had been working on an essay for this contest sponsored by Clean Teens, an antidrug organization. The winner would get their essay published in *Screenager* magazine. I'd heard the essay in different stages about twenty times. But I wasn't allowed to say no. Talk about trapped.

"Sure," I said.

Jen took a piece of paper out of her notebook. She cleared her throat. "'Drug addiction is the plague of our generation. It preys on the weak and the vulnerable. It splits apart families and drives a wedge between friends. . . .'"

I zoned again. Nicole had mentioned she was a blonde. But did she have short or long hair? Was it curly or straight?

After a few minutes, Jen looked over the paper at me. "You're not listening!"

"Sure I am!" I said. "Of course I am. Drug

addiction is the plague of our generation. For sure."

Jen sighed. "What's wrong with it?"

"Nothing."

"Tell me," Jen said. "Really. I can take constructive criticism."

"Well," I said. I sensed a potential minefield here. Jen isn't great at taking criticism. She could be touchy. So I carefully put down one foot and tested the ground. . . .

"It lacks something," I said.

"Something?" Jen asked, leaning forward. "Like what?"

"Like . . . zing," I said.

"Zing?"

I inched the next foot into the minefield. "It's kind of . . . boring," I said.

Boom! I'd just blown sky high.

Color rushed into Jen's face. "Boring?"

"It sounds kind of like a term paper," I said. "Written by a person with no personality."

"This is *constructive* criticism?" Jen asked, her voice rising to a squeak. "Why don't you just take a knife and cut me, Jonah!"

"You said you could take it!" I shot back. "I'm just trying to help you—"

"Well, this isn't help," Jen said, gathering her papers. "I didn't realize I had such a lack of *zip*."

"I didn't say you lacked zip," I pointed out. "I said you lacked *zing*. You're the zippiest girl I know—"

"Now I'm *zippy*," Jen said. "Gee, thanks—"

"But you have to admit, you have a real up close and personal knowledge of this whole drug thing, and you're writing about it like it's some kind of survey," I said.

Jen's lips pressed together. "That's mean, Jonah. You know Scott is better now—"

"I know! That's what I'm saying! You went through this whole awful freaky period, and you're acting like you don't know anything about it firsthand!" I said. I wished I hadn't opened my mouth at all. If Jen is closemouthed about her father, she eats paste when it comes to her brother. She and Scott had been superclose before he'd become a flake. She'd really needed him when their dad left, and instead, he'd gotten all sullen and mean, and then he'd started orbiting the planet. Then, as soon as he was off drugs and acting halfway normal, he'd split for college.

"I guess I'd better go," I said, even though it wasn't nearly time.

"Yeah, I guess," Jen said. She looked as though she was trying not to cry.

I felt pretty awful running out. But once I hit

the open air, I felt better. Jen and I would make up. We always did. And I had another girl waiting for me.

As soon as I got home, I clicked on my mailbox icon, and sure enough, Nicole had come through.

Dear JonBoy,

Okay, here's the real me. Remember our deal. If you're disappointed, just don't tell me. I have my pride, baby.

Love,

gemini.7

Gemini.7 was Nicole's Internet address. Gemini is her last name. I started the download function, and I waited.

Slowly, Nicole's image formed on my screen. Her blond hair was long and straight. Parted on the side, it kind of flipped over one eye. She was wearing faded jeans, and her legs went on forever. She smiled at the camera as if to say, *I'm yours, Jonah.*

In short, she was a total and complete knockout.

And there was only one word to describe what she did to me.

Va-va-va-voom-de-ay!

3//virtual love reality

Disappointed? Are you crazy? First of all, you're gorgeous, I wrote that night to Nicole. *You've gotta know that.*

Don't you know by now that all girls are insecure? Nicole wrote back. *I guess I'm just looking for someone who likes the real me.*

I like the real you, I wrote.

It sure helped that the "real Nicole" just happened to be a perfect 10. Talk about dream girls!

I'm really glad I can picture you now when I think about you, I added. I had to wait a few minutes for her words to flash onscreen.

I'm glad you think about me, she wrote. *I think about you, too. All the time.*

A girl who looks like Nicole Gemini thought about me all the time. If this is a dream, please don't wake me!

Nicole sent me the same picture through snail mail. It was small enough to fit in my wallet, but big enough to include every curve. I promised myself I wouldn't show it to anyone. But I was dying to show it to Matt. Tell me I'm wrong, but it's way too much to ask a teenage guy to keep a photo like that under wraps.

Of course, showing it to Matt meant that I had to tell him how I'd met Nicole online. Which meant I had to come clean about my cyber girls.

I told him the story as we were shooting hoops in his backyard. Before I could even get the picture out of my knapsack, Matt started grilling me about why I was "dating" through the computer.

"I'm not dating," I said. "I'm just talking to girls." I threw him an underhand pass.

"You're *flirting* with them," Matt said.

"So?" I said over the sound of his dribbling. "It's just through a computer, Matt. What's the big deal?"

"The big deal is, you're with *Jen*," Matt said. "If you have a steady girl, then you shouldn't flirt with other people." He did a layup. *Swish*.

I went in for the rebound. "I'm not flirting with girls at school, or with Jenny's friends," I said. "I'm talking to a girl in Hawaii!"

Matt shrugged again. "Whatever."

Now I was getting steamed. I drove under the

basket, reversed direction, and shot. The ball bounced off the rim and Matt caught it in midair.

"Anyway, look who's talking," I said. "You're the one who's trading dates for grades. I don't see you turning down Miss Pout of Milleridge High, Alison Potasher."

Now it was Matt's turn to get angry. I could tell by the way he slammed the ball against the driveway. "Listen, hotshot," he said. "The reason I chase after girls is that I don't *have* a girl like Jen. But you do! So why do you want to mess it up?"

"I'm not messing it up!" I said. I snatched the ball away from him. "I'm just visiting a chat room, not dating cheerleaders behind her back!"

Matt swept his curly hair off his forehead. "Look, just forget it."

"Matt, Nicole and I are just friends."

"Okay," he said.

"I'm not going to hurt Jen," I said.

"Okay," he said. "So?"

"So?"

Matt sighed. "So show me the picture."

I tossed him the ball, then reached into the back pocket of my jeans and took it out. I handed it to Matt.

Matt let out a long whistle. "Whoa," he said. "I see what you mean."

"The mold from which all dream girls are made," I said.

"So what does she see in you?" Matt asked, handing the photograph back to me.

"Thanks a lot," I said.

"Of course, she hasn't actually *met* you," Matt mused. He dribbled the ball. "I notice you're not breaking a leg to send her *your* picture. She probably doesn't realize that you're such a geek."

"Sez you," I said. Okay, I'm not the most studly guy in the world. I have brown hair and brown eyes, and if a word popped into someone's brain to describe me, it would probably be "ordinary." But did my best friend have to point it out?

"You're not exactly Brad Pitt yourself," I said.

Matt threw the ball at me harder than he had to, but I caught it and fired it back. He went in for a layup, and when the ball swished in I yelled, "Whoa—lucky shot!"

Matt smirked at me. "Some luck, shorty. Doncha wish you had some?"

We were friends again.

Sports. They smooth out anything. Where would I be without them?

A couple of nights later, when I clicked into the chat room, I saw AMbergrl had logged on. I hadn't talked to Amber in a while, so I said hello right away.

Where have you been, grrl? I typed out.

I shld ask ze same, bro, she wrote back. *As for moi, I've been MUDding like crazy.*

Amber is seriously devoted to MUDs—multi-user dimension fantasy games on the Net. Quite a few regulars in my fave chat room had a serious MUD Jones.

I knew that Nicole had played Amber's favorite MUD, Planet FamZoo, also known as PlanFam. Amber had tried to explain the game to me several times. When you sign on, you are transported to this weird, futuristic/prehistoric planet that is ruled by Families. There is an intense power structure among the different Fams, and usually several wars are going on. The deal is, though, that nobody can kill anybody else. You can just form alliances.

There are a couple of different ways to play the game. You can remain independent, you can try to break off and form your own Fam, or you can try to make a bunch of power moves in order to align yourself to the most powerful Fam.

It all sounded confusing to me, but the players take it superseriously. Maybe you have to be there.

Wazzup with you, J-Boy? Amber wrote.

Just then I saw Nicole's name pop up on the

list. She usually signed on around this time.

I've been hitting the books, big time, I wrote. *Finals coming up. Trig and I are not pals. Looks like I'm heading for summer school.*

Major drag, Amber wrote. *Need an online tutor?*

But before I could answer, Nicole joined the conversation. *JonBoy, join me in the hall?* she asked. That meant she wanted to have a private chat.

I typed out a *buh-bye* to Amber and moved into the private cyber hallway.

I've been trying to figure out a way to meet, Nicole wrote. *Are you into it?*

Sure, I answered. *But it's Mission Impossible. I'm saving up for a used car, but until I find something, I'm w/o wheels. Not that my parents would let me drive to Massachusetts, anyway. And then there's that summerlong date with trig.*

Don't worry, you won't have to go to summer school, Nicole wrote. *And I'm thinking of a plan for us. I have to meet you, Jonah!!!!!!!!!!*

I counted the exclamation points. Ten. Tell me I'm wrong, but that seemed like a good sign.

So I upped the ante to eleven: *I feel the same way!!!!!!!!!!!*

Finals were brutal. I was absolutely, one hundred percent positive that my trig teacher designed the exam specifically to torture me. It was a sweat-fest. I needed to ace it in order to pull my grade up to a C. The chances of that were about as good as me playing for the Bulls next season.

Summer school couldn't be *that* bad. I told myself that every day as the last day of school approached.

But when I got my report card, I nearly fell over my desk. Not only did I pass, I got a B in trig! I stared at the grade, not believing it. Maybe it was a D, only there was an ink spot in the middle that made it *look* like a B.

I checked the card again to make sure it was my card. Sure enough, there was my name: JONAH LANIER. But what if Mrs. Abalene had entered the wrong grade? I'd better keep a low profile for the rest of the day.

Jen had a different homeroom, and as soon as the bell rang, she hurried to my classroom.

"Well?" she asked.

I handed her the card. "Read it and weep."

"Oh, Jonah," she sighed. "I'm really sor—"

Jen's head snapped up again. "You got a B!"

I nodded happily. "Do you think I was touched by an angel?"

She peered down at it. "Unless that's an ink spot, and it's really a D . . . no, it's a B." Jen bit her lip. "Do you think Mrs. Abalene entered the wrong grade?"

"Thanks a lot, Jen," I said, even though she had read my very own thoughts. "Thanks for the confidence."

"It's not that, Jonah, it's just that . . . well, you were so positive you didn't do well on the exam," Jen said. "And we studied together the night before, so I know how behind you were. . . ."

"So I pulled it out at the last minute," I said. Even though everything Jen said was true, I couldn't help feeling irritated. "Is that so unbelievable?"

If I expected Jen to backtrack and apologize, I didn't know Jenny Malone. Her hazel eyes shot sparks at me.

"What's up with you these days?" she asked, handing me back the card. "I can't say anything right anymore. What's your problem?"

I stuffed the card in my backpack. "I'm human, aren't I? I'm allowed to be in a bad mood once in a while."

"Sure," Jen said. "But you don't have to make a habit of it."

I slung my backpack over my shoulder. "Sorry," I said. "If I'm that hard to be around, maybe you should leave me alone."

Jen's face was flushed. "Maybe I should."

I shrugged. She tossed her hair. It was our usual standoff.

I knew she was waiting for me to apologize. When I didn't, she spun around and stalked away.

You passed? Awesome! I knew you could do it, Jonah! With your mind, you could do anything.

Now that's what a guy likes to hear. Nicole expected the best from me, instead of being surprised by it like Jen was.

But I'd been thinking about something all the way home from school. Nicole was a major hacker. Could she have broken into the school computer system? She had said that I wouldn't have to go to summer school before I even took the test.

Nicole, don't get me wrong. I'm happy about my grade. But you wouldn't have . . . given me a little help, would you?

What do you mean, Jonah? Nicole asked.

Hacker help, I said. *Because cheating just isn't my style.*

Nicole's words flowed across the screen:

Of course I didn't do anything! You got that grade on your own. When are you going to trust how smart you are?

I have to say, I am not one to underestimate myself. As a matter of fact, I'm as realistic about my ability to conquer trig as I am about the accuracy of my jump shot. I knew there was no way I had aced that final.

But I told myself that anything could happen. I *wanted* to believe Nicole more than anything. I wanted to be the guy she said I was. I wanted to believe that I was smart enough not to study all semester, then ace a final.

So I did.

4//summer daze

Early the next morning, while I was chugging orange juice from the carton, there was a knock at the door. It was Jen, carrying a plate full of blueberry muffins.

"Don't get excited, they're not homemade," she told me. "I got them at the bakery."

"They are still an excellent peace offering," I approved. I snatched one. "Come on in. Want some juice?" I handed her the carton.

Jen made a face at it, then went to the cupboard for glasses. "I felt awful last night, Jonah," she said, her face in the cupboard. "I hate it when we fight."

Whoa. Major guilt pang. I'd been too busy chatting with Nicole to feel bad about fighting with Jen. When we'd signed off, we'd even bracketed each other's names with hugs:

{{{Nicole}}} {{{{Jonah}}}}

If you hugged another girl with parentheses, did that mean you were cheating on your girlfriend?

"It was my fault," I said. "You were right. I *have* been a total crank monster lately. I guess it was school pressure or something."

Jen looked relieved as she plopped down in the chair and poured juice for us. "Good. So that's settled." She pushed a glass toward me, then leaned her chin on her hand and smiled. "Because I was freaked out last night. I've had two awful summers in a row. First my dad left, then Scott fell apart. I really want to coast this summer. Just have fun, hang out."

I nodded. Last summer was when Scott went into drug rehab. I think Mrs. Malone and Jen held their breath for three entire months.

"Your wish is my command," I said. "One perfect summer, coming up."

A bunch of the guys had decided to kick off summer with a basketball game. I headed over to the courts with Matt. As soon as we got there, Tommy Brandon yelled, "Hey, here comes Lanier!" at me across the court. He is five feet eleven inches of studly obnoxious handsomeness, and even though he isn't a bad guy, Matt and I aren't exactly his best pals. So why he was greeting me like a long-lost cousin I had no idea.

He tucked the ball under one muscled arm in a cutoff sweatshirt. "Hey, I hear you have some hot cyber babe wired to your modem," he said.

I gave Matt a sour look. He is A number one when it comes to best-friendhood. But when it comes to keeping secrets, he might as well have his own talk show.

"I just told *one* person," Matt said to me defensively.

I rolled my eyes. "Was it Oprah?"

"Come on, Lanier," Tommy Brandon said. "Let's see the picture."

"Matt says she's supermodel material," Jeremy Sugarman said.

All the guys crowded around me. Suddenly, I was Mr. Popular. I reached into the back pocket of my shorts, where I kept the picture of Nicole. I took it with me wherever I went now, mostly because I have the nosiest brother and sister in the world. Nothing is safe in my room. And I mean nothing. Once Annie cut up my underpants for doll bandages and brought them to school.

I slowly pulled out the picture. Then I held it facedown for a minute. Their tongues were practically wagging. I enjoyed the moment.

"Come on, Jonah!" Greg Villanova said.

I handed the picture to Jeremy.

"Whoa," he said reverently.

Greg grabbed it. "Wow," he said.

He handed it to Sam Posen, who handed it down the line. Finally, it reached the hand of Tommy Brandon. He stared down at it for a long minute.

I waited for the hearty Brandon masculine approval. It would last me all the way through senior year. I would be a member of the stud farm, for sure.

Suddenly, Tommy made this obnoxious hooting noise. "You've got to be kidding me, Lanier," he said. "You think *this* is your cyber girl? Dream on!"

"It's Nicole," I said. "She sent it to me."

"Oh, I'm sure she sent it," Tommy said, waving the photograph. "But that doesn't mean it's *her*. This is a picture of some model. Let's face it—why would a girl who looks like *this* need to troll for dates on the Internet? Nicole is probably your typical cyber geek. Scrawny and pasty, with inch-thick glasses and no personality. Some dream girl," Tommy said. He tossed the photo back to me. "Try nightmare!"

Tommy dribbled the ball and tossed it to Greg. The rest of the guys moved toward the basket.

"Talk about nightmares," Matt said, jerking his chin toward Tommy. "At least it's summer, and your contact with Brandon will be minimal."

I put the picture back in my pocket. "It *is* her, Matt. I know it is."

Matt shrugged. "What difference does it make? You're never going to meet her."

"Right," I said.

The trouble was, lately Nicole had been harping on arranging some way to meet. I went along, because the chances of hooking up were mighty slim. But Nicole wasn't giving up.

Maybe sending those eleven exclamation points hadn't been such a hot idea, after all.

I had two weeks until my job started, and I had planned to cram every bit of summer fun I could into them. Swimming in the still-cold Delaware River. Softball games in the riverside park. Monday night concerts at the band shell with Jen. And I'd planned to see every block-buster summer movie on the day it premiered.

Well, so much for plans. Instead of movies and sports, I talked to Nicole. When I woke up, there was always an e-mail waiting for me. I answered it before breakfast. Then, I had this major summer chore of refinishing some old fur-niture for the "library" Dad was creating out of an old storage room upstairs. I'd take a break before lunch and check my e-mail again. There was always a reply from Nicole.

In the afternoons, I usually told Jen that I had to work refinishing furniture. Instead, I chatted with Nicole.

And then, after dinner, when Jen would call and say a bunch of kids were going to the mall, or ask if I wanted to take a walk along the river, I'd find some excuse to say no. Then I'd talk to Nicole.

It wasn't that I was trying to avoid Jen. It was that Nicole was so . . . irresistible. She even worked the Internet for me and found me the absolutely perfect used car. My dad drove me over to Milford to buy it.

I stopped visiting the chat room completely. Why listen to a bunch of people gassing on and on about their favorite movies when I could talk to Nicole?

She was interested in everything about me and my family. She even asked lots of concerned questions about my dad, who was currently acting like a bear with rabies. Dad was doing the corporate cutthroat gig with this rival at work. They were up for the same promotion, and Dad was afraid this guy would get it and then fire him. Let me tell you, the Lanier household was feeling the heat.

One night, when Mom called us in for supper, Dad said he just didn't feel like eating. He poured a bowl of Annie's Frosted Flakes and took it into the den. It was the most pathetic thing I'd ever seen in my life.

Annie's big caramel brown eyes grew even rounder. She stopped kicking my chair and looked at Mom. "What's wrong with Daddy?"

Mom's smile was more like a muscle twitch. "He's fine, sweetie. He just doesn't feel well."

Annie's lip wobbled. "Will he eat all my cereal?"

"Shut up, squirt," my brother, Dewey, told her fiercely. But he looked scared, not angry.

Mom didn't even snap at Dewey for calling his sister a name. "Eat your peas," she told us, but you could tell she wasn't thinking about us at all. We were having broccoli.

I wrote an e-mail to Nicole about the awful dinner, then felt totally stupid. Quickly, I fired another one:

N,

Sorry to rag on you about my dad. The Frosted Flakes just got to me, I guess. It must have been total boredom to read.

J

I got a response in about five minutes.

J,

Don't apologize to me for being concerned about your dad. I totally understand. At least, I'd like to understand. When your parents are dead, you want to hear about other families.

Nicole's parents were dead! I didn't even know! Suddenly, I realized that we talked about *me* all the time. Which is not exactly a compelling subject. Unless you're me, of course.

That night, in our private chat room, Nicole told me how her parents had died in a plane crash. They'd been in a small plane on a runway when another plane landed and smashed into them. Nicole had stayed home from the trip because of the flu. Now she lives with her grandparents.

I guess they love me, she wrote. *But they have these really busy lives. They take golf vacations every couple of months. And they're totally into bridge, so they're out about three nights a week. I'm alone a lot. That's why the computer became my friend. If I didn't have my laptop, I'd go crazy.*

I knew how gorgeous Nicole was. I knew how much fun she could be, and how generous. But for the first time, my dream girl turned into a person. And I realized that she could just about break my heart.

One night, Nicole sent me an e-mail that just said:

Dear Jonah,

I've figured it out! Meet me at 5 p.m.

When I signed on, Nicole told me that she'd figured out a way for us to meet. Her grandmother was treating her to a weekend in Boston. They were supposed to shop and go to museums, but Nicole was positive her grandmother would dump her at the hotel so that she could visit friends and play bridge. All I had to do was convince my parents that we should take a short vacation trip to Boston at the same time.

Tell them you're taking American history next year and it would be really educational, Nicole wrote. *Parents dig that stuff.*

It wasn't a bad idea. And that way, I could meet Nicole away from the home turf. Jen would never know.

I'll give it my best shot, I told her.

You had to time things with parentals. You waited for the moment when they were completely relaxed, or maybe almost asleep while they were watching TV. And then you pounced.

The problem was, Dad wasn't doing much relaxing these days. I had to tackle him at his caffeine-charged worst—breakfast time.

While he chugged his coffee, I droned on about how much I wanted to go to Boston and how it was such an educational city. I talked about Paul Revere's ride and the Liberty Bell. I didn't think he was listening to me, but I should never underestimate my dad.

"The Liberty Bell is in Philadelphia," he said. "We've taken you to see it."

"Right. I knew that. But all the other Revolutionary stuff is in Boston. You know what a buff I am."

He raised an eyebrow. "I must have missed this fervor for our historical heritage, Jonah."

"It's a new Jones, Dad," I said. "It's replaced basketball in my heart."

"I'm shocked," he said dryly.

"Anyway, Boston is crammed with history. We could walk the Freedom Trail, and go to North Church and hang a couple lanterns . . . you know."

Dad put down his coffee cup. He'd been working on a report until late the night before. He looked like he needed another twelve pots of coffee to get going.

"Jonah, I'm in advertising," he said. "I recognize a hard sell when I see one."

So maybe I was coming on a little strong. "Will you just think about it?" I pleaded.

He stood up and straightened his tie. "It's not a bad idea. Maybe a long weekend."

"You could use it, Dad," I said.

One corner of his mouth lifted. "An interest in history *and* a concern for my well-being. Is it Father's Day?"

I ran upstairs to send Nicole an e-mail saying there was a chance Dad and Mom would okay the trip. A letter was waiting for me from Amber. I hadn't heard from her in weeks.

J,

what's with that psycho cyber witch gemini girlfriend of yours? tell her to lay off! if I were you, I'd be careful. if you want to join the human race again, drop into the chat room.

A

Frowning, I stared at the message. Cyber witch? Did she mean Nicole? Sweet, vulnerable, lonely Nicole?

No way!

5//flaming

When I hinted to Nicole that Amber could be slightly ticked off at her, Nicole fired back an e-mail.

She's the one who's a wacko. All I did was ask if you'd go into a private chat room, and the next thing I know, she flamed me! Everyone is jealous of us, Jonah. We're soul mates, and people just can't stand it.

So Nicole claimed that Amber flamed her first. For any non–cyber freaks in the audience, "flaming" is like calling someone names in the school yard, except you can be even nastier in cyber space since you aren't face-to-face. You can bombard their mailbox with messages about how lame they are. I couldn't see Amber doing that to Nicole, but I couldn't imagine Nicole doing it to Amber, either. Then again, they're girls. They're from another planet. Not even a trig whiz like *moi* can figure them out.

I have to admit, though, that there was a tiny

part of me that got a kick out of two girls cat-fighting over my person. Okay. Maybe not so tiny.

I was heading home one day when I saw my dad standing in the middle of the lawn, staring up at the house. He had a weird expression on his face. I checked to make sure that an alien spacecraft wasn't landing on our roof.

"Dad? You okay?"

He nodded, but it was like he hadn't heard me at all. That's when it hit me. *He got fired.*

"We need a new roof," he said.

"I know, Dad," I said gently.

Mom came out on the porch. "Michael?" she called to my dad. "Are you okay?" Her voice was soft, just like mine. We were both freaked.

"Amy," Dad said. "We can fix the roof."

Mom's voice was patient, as if she were talking to Annie when she had a fever. "What was that, sweetheart?"

"I got the promotion," Dad said.

Mom and I froze. Then Mom jumped down the steps two at a time and threw herself at Dad. They hugged each other with big, goofy grins on their faces.

"Why didn't you call?" Mom said. "I could have bought champagne—"

"I wanted to call," Dad said at the same time. "But I wanted to see your face when I told you—"

They jumped up and down, holding on to each other's arms. I swear. Parentals are children with credit cards.

Dad reached out and grabbed me, including me in the hug. "I've been a bear all week," he said. "Sorry, Jonah."

"It's okay, Dad," I said. "I didn't notice."

"Right," he said.

"But if you want to buy me a Porsche . . ."

We all laughed.

"How did it happen?" Mom asked as we headed toward the house. "You thought Dubinski was going to get it."

"It was the strangest thing," Dad said, shaking his head. "Dubinski wrote this memo to himself, listing all the objectives he had if he got the promotion. In it he critiqued management decisions over the past year and even plotted out how he'd get his boss fired and take over *that* position in six months. The memo got sent out to company e-mail by mistake. Every single person in the company read it. Including Mr. Blake, who Dubinski was plotting to get fired. Dubinski was forced to resign, and Blake gave me the job."

Dad paused with his hand on the screen door. "The gods of cyber space were watching out for me, I guess."

I patted Dad on the back, hoping to dislodge his stunned expression. "May the force be with you, Pops," I said.

Dad took the family out to our favorite Italian restaurant to celebrate. I brought leftovers back to Jen and told her all about it.

"That's justice for you," Jen said. "The guy deserved to get nailed. I'm glad your dad won."

"Here's the best part," I said. "Dad and Mom got all goony at dinner, talking about their honeymoon in Italy. And they want to take all of us there this summer!"

"Awesome!" Jen said. "Europe! You are so lucky!"

"We're going to Venice and Florence and Rome, for sure. But then Mom started talking about Paris—"

"Paris," Jen breathed. "*Ooo-la-la!*"

"So they decided to go to France, too," I said.

"You have to take lots of pictures," Jen said. Her hazel eyes were shining. She looked so pretty. *Who needs Nicole?* I thought. "And send me postcards, so I can have French and Italian stamps. Oh, I know—you can keep a journal, so you'll remember every detail. I hate it when people get back from trips and can't remember stuff."

"I'll remember everything," I said. "Just for you."

Jen put her hand over mine and squeezed it. "I'm glad you came over tonight and told me," she said. "It's been kind of weird lately. You've been so busy with your dad's furniture. I guess I thought we'd be spending more time together before we start work."

Guilt zinged me like a bad tooth. "I know," I said. "I guess since Dad was so freaked in general, I wanted to do something for him."

"I can understand that," Jen said. "Totally." She played with my fingers. "I guess we won't be going to the cottage this summer."

We had this lake cabin in the foothills of the Poconos. It was basically a shack, with three tiny bedrooms and a sagging porch. Mom and Dad usually rented it out in July, but we always went there for two weeks in August. Jen had come for the past three summers, and we'd had a blast.

"Dad said we could squeeze in a weekend before we leave," I said.

Jen smiled. "Good. Because I'm going to cream you this year at badminton."

"You and what army?" I said.

"My right and my left," Jen said, giggling. She flexed a muscle. "So watch out. I'm going to get some real muscles this summer from working on the grounds crew."

"Badminton doesn't take muscles," I said. "It takes finesse. Strategy."

"Mmmm," Jen said. "That must be why Annie and I beat you last summer."

"The sun was in my eyes," I said.

Jen laughed. "Tell your story walking, Jones. It's late, and I promised Mom I'd come up to bed soon."

"Nobody appreciates me," I said loftily. I stood and fished in my pocket for my keys. "I might as well go home," I said, bringing out my keys with a flourish. "At least there I have leftovers to console me."

"You brought *me* the leftovers, remember?" Jen said, laughing. She bent over. "And you dropped something, Sherlock."

It was the picture of Nicole. It must have fluttered out when I took out my keys! Quickly, I moved to put my foot on it, but Jen was faster. She picked it up.

"Jonah? Who is *this*?"

She didn't ask me in an accusing way. More like a curious way. That's because she trusted me. Talk about guilt!

"That's a very good question," I said.

I guess I sounded nervous. Jen looked at me sharply. "Do you know this girl?"

I should have just told her the truth. Because the whole thing was completely innocent. I'd never even met Nicole. She was just a cyber buddy. I pictured the words coming out of my mouth. Of course Jen would understand.

Then again, the sun could rise in the west tomorrow.

"She's my cousin," I blurted.

"Your cousin from Wisconsin? I thought she was twelve." Jen eyed the photograph again.

"From France," I said. "Her name is Nicole. Dad wrote to these cousins in France, and they sent pictures. They live in Paris. That's where we're going to stay. With them."

"Didn't your dad just decide to go to France tonight? And she doesn't look French," Jen said, staring at the picture.

"What does that mean?" I said. "Do you want her to wear a beret and smoke a cigarette?"

"She's wearing Levi's," Jen said.

"They have Levi's in France," I said. "They *love* Levi's there. As a matter of fact, we're taking some over as presents when we go. . . ." I remembered what Dad had said about a hard sell, so I shut up.

Jen was barely listening, anyway. She was staring at the picture. "She's pretty," she said. "But her expression is kind of weird. Like she knows she's pretty, and she knows that you know. You know?"

"No." I took the picture back and stuffed it in my pocket. "Anyway, you don't have to be jealous. She's my *cousin*."

Jen gave me a funny look. "I'm not jealous," she said. "Why should I be?"

"No reason," I said. "No reason at all."

WHAT ABOUT BOSTON? Nicole typed back when I told her about the trip to Europe. *I thought we could finally be together!!!!*

I've been to Europe. Believe me, it's no big deal. It's PEOPLE who are important. Not PLACES. I know I'm being selfish. It's just that I'll miss you so much. {{{{{{Jonah}}}}}}!!!! WE BELONG TOGETHER!!!!!!

I have to admit I was taken aback by Nicole's reaction. She used uppercase letters, which in cyber space is the equivalent of shouting. I'd never had a girl get so upset over me before.

After all, Jen hadn't said she'd miss me during my exotic vacation. She was just looking forward to the stamps.

When my dad got his credit card bill, I shouldn't have been surprised that my online bill had tripled. I'd been talking to Nicole for hours and hours for weeks. The problem was, I couldn't pay it. And that was the agreement with my dad.

"The service is supposed to go to a flat rate soon," I said helpfully.

"Great," Dad said. "Terrific. So when you finish paying off this bill, you can sign on again."

"But, Dad—"

He looked over the bill at me. "Yes?"

Suddenly, I felt that reminding him that he'd just gotten a promotion and could afford to be generous wouldn't go over well.

"Nothing," I mumbled.

"I'll pay this so that I'm not behind with my bills," Dad said. "But, Jonah, you have to pay me back. Until then, your online service is cut off for the duration."

I made a few quick calculations. Considering the size of my savings account, which was zip thanks to my new car, against the size of my paycheck, which suddenly seemed puny, "the duration" could last at least a month. Maybe six weeks. And then we'd be taking off for Europe.

In short, I'd be offline for the whole summer.

Nicole! She had freaked at the thought of me offline for two weeks. What would she say when she heard about this?

6//almost normal

That morning, Nicole was quiet for so long that I thought she'd turned off her computer. But after I prompted her:

Nicole?????????

She answered:

I'll wait for you.

We didn't spend very long saying good-bye. I didn't want to run up any more charges.

I expected to feel totally bummed when I switched off the computer. That I'd feel weird, and spacey, like I was cut off from everything. But I didn't get a chance, because Jen called.

"It's gorgeous out," she said. "Can you leave the furniture stripping for once and go swimming?"

"Meet you outside in fifteen minutes," I said.

I'd taken Jen for a ride in my car when I first got it. But this was the first time we'd really cruised, with all the windows open, the sun shining, and a whole summer day ahead of us. We went to the river and paddled around on inner tubes. We listened to music and splashed water at each other and caught rays on the big rocks by the shore. Jen had packed chicken salad sandwiches and sodas in a cooler, and we had a huge bag of potato chips. It was an unbelievably majestic day.

I realized that I'd been inside the house for weeks because of that computer. And Nicole. And I'd missed stuff. I'd missed the river getting warm enough to swim in. I'd missed how Jen's legs were getting tan, and seeing that there were now eleven freckles on her nose.

I counted them solemnly while she tilted her face to the sun.

"No, wait—twelve," I said. "There's one over here by your ear."

"You are a complete and utter weirdsmobile," Jen said, smiling with her eyes closed.

I touched my fingertip to a couple of the freckles. "Do you know, if I traced these, I could make an isosceles triangle? If I used this one by your left eye . . ."

Jen batted my hand away. "How do you know what an isosceles triangle is, anyway? You practically flunked geometry."

"Hey, I got a C."

"Only because I saved your sorry butt," Jen said, opening one eye.

I squinted at her face. "I could even bisect it," I said. "Let's see now—the square of A plus B cubed—"

"Don't even try," Jen said, laughing.

"Equals C," I said, but I had to stop, because Jen leaned over and kissed me. It was probably just to shut me up, but I'd take what I could get.

And I didn't miss Nicole at all.

Over the next few days, I caught up with summer. Jen and I hit the movies, and the mall, and went swimming every day. We had killer Ping-Pong games with Matt. We cruised up and down the river road in my car with all the windows down and the radio on.

Jen bought this emerald blouse that made her eyes look woodsy green. When she kissed me good night, there was nowhere in the world I'd rather have been than in Milleridge, Pennsylvania. And no girl I'd rather have been with than Jennifer Ashley Malone.

The summer had shifted into neutral, and it was fine by me.

Late one afternoon, I dropped Jen at her house before pulling into my driveway. She paused with her hand on the door.

"The magic number is three," she said.

I knew what she meant right away. In only

three days, we had to start our summer jobs.

"I know," I said. "I wish we could goof off all summer."

"But it will be nice to have a paycheck," Jen said. "Hey, I have an idea. Tomorrow, let's drive upriver and rent inner tubes. It's supposed to be almost eighty degrees. It'll be a perfect day to do a river trip."

We'd done the trip at least once every summer. We'd float downriver for hours, going through tiny rapids with sodas tied onto the inner tubes in case we got thirsty. When we got hot, we'd roll off the tubes and swim.

"Sounds fantastic," I said. "I'll pick you up at ten."

Jen kissed me swiftly, then hurried up the walk to her house. It was her night to cook dinner. I drove the short distance to my house and pulled in the driveway. As I turned off the ignition, my mom came running out of the house. She had one arm in her denim jacket, and it flew behind her as she raced to her car.

"Jonah, you have to pull out," she said. "I have . . . to . . . ." Tears spurted out of her eyes.

"Mom, what is it?" I said.

"There's been an accident," she said, her voice shaking. "It's Dad. Someone ran him off the road. He's in the hospital!"

7 // smashup

Mom was a mess, so I drove to the hospital while Dewey watched Annie. At first, I wasn't allowed to see Dad. They let Mom into the emergency room, and she was gone for about ten minutes. When she came back out, she didn't come toward me. She leaned her forehead against the wall right outside the swinging doors. Her shoulders shook.

I hurried over to her. I didn't know if my heart was beating too fast, or not beating at all. I'd never felt so scared. "Mom? Is Dad okay?"

Mom straightened up immediately. She tried to smile. "He's okay, Jonah. Really. I mean, he'll *be* okay. His face got cut a little bit, and it shook me." She reached out and hugged me, hard. "He'll be okay," she repeated.

She wiped her eyes. "I'd better call Dewey. Dad's going to be in the hospital for a couple of days. So we'll all have to pull together, okay?" She squeezed my shoulder. "I'm going to have to count on you. Maybe Jen can help you with dinners and stuff."

"Mom, don't worry about it," I said. "I'll take care of everything."

She hugged me again. "I know, sweetie."

"Did he see who did it?" I said. "Was it an accident?"

Mom frowned. "He's not sure. This car came out of nowhere. A maroon car with a black top, and out-of-state plates. It forced him off the road. It happened so fast that Dad never got a look at the driver. The police are looking for the car, but without a license number . . ." Mom shrugged.

"I guess it doesn't matter," I said. "It was probably just some weirdo."

She nodded. "Dad's going to be okay. That's the important thing."

When I told her, Jen's face went still and white. "Is he okay?"

"He's okay," I assured her. "He has to stay in the hospital for a couple of days, though."

Tears formed in Jen's eyes. She is really close to both my parents. "What can I do? Can I see him?"

"Maybe in a day or two. He's still in intensive care," I said. It felt so weird to say the words "intensive care" and know they had to do with my dad.

"Oh, Jonah. I'm so sorry." Jen put her arms around me and rested her head against my shoulder.

I felt as though I'd been running on a weird frequency all day long. Everything had looked so different. Even familiar things, like my house, looked strange suddenly. But Jen looked familiar and comforting. I leaned against her, too.

The house felt empty without Mom and Dad. Mom took off a few days from work. She was at the hospital almost all day and through the evening. Dewey, Annie, and I went to the afternoon visiting hours. Dad looked skinny in his hospital gown, and his hair was all flat from having a bandage near his ear and lying in bed all day.

"I know," he said to me. "Major pillow hair, right?"

"Major, Dad," I said.

"I love that show," Dad said.

So we were joking like everything was normal. But it wasn't.

Jen brought over this awesome baked manicotti that she makes. She stayed and read to Annie before she went to bed. But even Jen had to go home sometime. The nights felt so dark and lonely.

So I switched on my computer. To my surprise, my online service was still running. Dad must have forgotten to cancel it. I felt guilty using it, but I wanted to talk to Nicole. I did an online search, and she clicked into "instant message" right away. I told her what happened to my dad.

That's awful!!!! Are you okay????

I'm fine, I said. *I'm holding down the fort here at home. But it's weird having Dad in the hospital. The house feels really empty.*

I know how you feel, Nicole wrote. *After my parents died, I'd just walk through all the rooms. It would always be a surprise somehow that they weren't there.*

What a bonehead I was! Sure, my dad was in the hospital. But he was going to be okay. Nicole had had it much worse.

We talked for a long time that night. About parents, and families, and how you think they're a drag sometimes, but then suddenly they matter the most in the world.

I guess a part of me will always feel like something's missing, Nicole said. *For a while, I felt like I had a tattoo, right in the middle of my forehead. GIRL WITHOUT A FAMILY. I felt like even strangers could tell I was alone.*

You have me, I said.

Yes, Nicole wrote back. *I have you.*

Dad was in the hospital for five days, and it felt like forever.

"I'll be *paying* for it forever," Dad said. And this time, his laugh sounded real.

But finally, he was due to come home. Mom was going to the hospital alone, but Annie put up such a stink that Mom said she could go. Annie is a four-year-old bulldozer. Then Dewey wanted to go, too. And Dewey usually doesn't say much of anything.

So I said I'd stay home and get the house ready. We wanted it to look nice for Dad, and Mom had bought his favorite cold cuts and cheeses for lunch. I said I'd make up the platters and make a big pitcher of iced tea.

Major points with Mom.

So I played house that morning, and it was fun. I washed all the windows and opened the curtains so that the house was flooded with sunlight. I made the tea and arranged the provolone and Swiss cheese and the ham and salami on Mom's blue ceramic platter. I lined a basket with a linen napkin and filled it with the kaiser rolls Mom had bought. I did all the stuff I had seen Mom do before.

And then I waited. I knew Dad had to deal with insurance forms and stuff, so who knew when they'd arrive. But finally, I heard steps on the front porch. Which was funny, because I hadn't heard the car. I'd probably been listening too hard.

I hurried to the front door. "Welcome home!" I said, flinging it open.

But Dad wasn't standing there. Instead, a girl stood there. The sunlight hit her blond hair, and I suddenly found myself lost in a pair of deep, deep blue eyes. Her lips curved into an uncertain smile.

"Jonah?"

8//walking dream

She was like a walking dream. She wore a short white skirt and a flowery vintage shirt in pale yellow. I know vintage because my mom haunts secondhand clothing stores.

Standing in front of me now was a ray of sunlight. A human version of butterscotch ice cream with whipped cream.

It was a vision. And then the vision spoke again. "It's Nicole."

I was still doing my impersonation of a wax dummy. Nicole took a step backward. "I shouldn't have come."

I snapped out of it. This was no dream girl. This was a living, breathing knockout right on my very own porch. And her smile was just for me.

Eat your heart out, Tommy Brandon!

"Nicole!" I said quickly. "It's really you."

She gave a shy smile. "It's really me. I just felt awful, thinking about your dad. I thought you could use some support."

"I'm really glad to see you," I said.

Her blue eyes grew even brighter. "You are?"

"You bet," I said. "Come on in."

I led Nicole into the house. She looked around, her gaze taking everything in. Then she stopped and sighed.

"This is perfect. It's just like I imagined. Just like you said. It reminds me of my old house in Massachusetts. Where I lived with my parents." She ran a hand along the end of the sofa. "And the furniture is just like I pictured it, too. It makes you want to curl up on a rainy day and read—"

"Is that a nice way to say that it's shabby?" I teased.

"No," she said quickly, "that's not what I—" Then she saw I was kidding, and she laughed. "So you're funny in person, too. I'd better watch out."

Me too, boy. Because Nicole Gemini was just about the most gorgeous girl I've ever met.

"So how did you get here?" I asked. "I didn't see a car."

"I took the bus," Nicole said.

"From Boston?"

She smiled. "No. From Parson's Ford."

Parson's Ford is a tiny town a few miles downriver.

"What were you doing there?" I asked.

"Visiting my aunt Margaret May," Nicole

explained. "Aunt Mags. She invited me to visit. I knew it was in Pennsylvania, but I had no idea the town was so close to Milleridge. As soon as I found out, I had to come see you. Are you surprised?"

"Surprised? I'm delirious," I said. "Somebody wake me."

Nicole took a step toward me. "I know. It's a dream come true, isn't it?"

Okay, I have a girlfriend. But that doesn't mean I have experience with girls. In fact, it means the opposite. I have experience with *Jen*. I know her moods as well as my own. I know when I can tease her out of a bad mood, and when it's better not to try. When she's pretending to be happy, and when she really is. When she wants me to kiss her, and when she wants me to back off.

But when it comes to other girls, I'm clueless. Because right then, right there in my sunny living room, I could have sworn that Nicole wanted me to kiss her. And I'd just *met* her. Sort of.

I think my brain melted, because I just stood there. Nicole didn't move, either. She ducked her head and looked up at me, catching her teeth on her bottom lip. She must have aced Flirtation 101.

I was almost relieved when my parents chose that moment to burst through the door.

I gave Dad a hug and made the introductions

really fast, explaining that Nicole was a cyber buddy who just happened to be in town. Dewey's eyes nearly fell out of his head. He probably thought that girls who look like Nicole are all twenty-seven inches high, the size of our TV screen.

"Why don't you join us for lunch, Nicole?" Mom asked. It was a Mom thing. If we are within two hours of a meal, she always invites my friends to it. Which can be a complete pain if you've invited someone like nerdy Alan Wicklow over only because you wanted to pick his chemistry-infused brain. Then you had to watch him eat three helpings of your favorite eggplant parmigiana.

"That sounds great," Nicole said. "Thank you, Mrs. Lanier. And afterward, maybe Jonah can show me around Milleridge. I'm fascinated by all the old houses here."

Nicole followed my parents into the kitchen. She'd sure said the magic word in this house: "old." Annie was looking up at her as though she were an angel. And Dewey hadn't been able to stop staring at her. It looked as though Nicole was a hit with the Lanier clan. It was amazing how, within five minutes, she fit right in.

Of course I wanted to be alone with Nicole. And naturally, driving a gorgeous girl around in my car was not exactly unpleasant. But as I've mentioned, Milleridge is a small town. How would I be able to explain Nicole to Jen if someone saw us together?

So I showed Nicole everything she wanted to see. The high school, the park, my hangouts, Main Street. I just did it at about forty miles an hour.

"I love this town," Nicole said in a wistful voice as I drove as fast as I dared down Candlemaker Street. "It reminds me of all the good times in my life. My town has a redbrick library, just like yours. There's an inn where George Washington supposedly slept—didn't that guy ever sleep at home? And a Revolutionary War monument in the town square. And once this big developer wanted to build a mini mall and tear down the oldest building in town—it used to be a blacksmith's shop; then it became a bookstore. The whole town got together and told the guy to go back to Boston where he belonged." Nicole laughed.

"Milleridge is like that," I said. "We even kicked out McDonald's. The headline in the *Milleridge Daily* was 'McScram!'"

I drove down to the river. Luckily, none of my friends were swimming or hanging out there.

"This is so pretty," Nicole said. "Let's go for a walk!"

"No!" I shouted. Nicole flinched, and I quickly said, "I mean, your aunt must be worried about you."

"No," Nicole said. "I told her I might be gone all day. Do you want to get rid of me, Jonah?"

"Of course not," I said. "It's just that . . . there are better places to walk. There's a state park right up the road with all kinds of neat trails. . . ."

"Jonah, are you okay?" Nicole asked. "You seem kind of jumpy."

"I'm fine," I said. I pulled out of the parking space and headed up the river road. If I didn't get out of Jen territory, I would have a heart attack. At least Nicole wouldn't be visiting very long.

"So how long are you staying with your aunt?" I asked.

"All summer," Nicole trilled. "Isn't that great, Jonah?"

I gulped. "It's majestic," I said. All summer? How would I be able to hide Nicole from Jen?

"You're frowning," Nicole said. She threw me a trademark girl-pout. And I thought Alison Potasher was a pro.

She looked out the window. "I guess this was a mistake. You're just being polite. You drove through town at fifty miles an hour, practically.

I could tell you didn't want to be seen with me. You just want me to go away. I can always tell."

I looked over. A tear was slowly dripping down the perfect curve of Nicole's cheek. I felt like a low-down dirty dog.

I swung the car over, parking on the grass by the river. I turned to Nicole. "I don't want you to go away," I said.

She kept her head down, her shiny long hair hiding her face. "It's okay," she said. "I understand."

"No," I said. "You don't. You see . . . I kind of have a girlfriend."

Nicole's head jerked up. Her navy blue eyes blazed. "You *what*?"

"Her name is Jen," I said. "We've been together since seventh grade."

Nicole whipped her head back and looked out the window. I saw her shoulders rise and fall as she took a deep breath. "Of course you have a girlfriend," she said softly. She turned back and gave me a melting gaze. "I was just surprised for a minute. But it would be too strange if a guy like you hadn't been snatched up."

Okay. I know I'm not the Hunchback of Notre Dame. But I'm not exactly Tommy Brandon, either. It would make complete and utter sense to me if I hadn't been snatched up by anybody, ever.

She turned back to me. The sun lit her eyes, turning them a lighter, clearer blue. I felt like I was drowning. Happily.

"You don't want to upset Jen. I can understand that."

I nodded.

"Or hurt her."

I nodded again. "She's a fantastic person. She—"

Nicole interrupted me. "I'm sure she is. But she's not your soul mate, Jonah. Is she."

It wasn't a question. And the beam of her eyes held me spellbound. I shook my head again, slowly.

She leaned forward, just a fraction of an inch from my face. I could feel her breath. "You have to tell her," she whispered. "It's the right thing to do. You can't lead her on."

"I don't know if—"

"Tell her," she said, moving even closer toward me. She said the words right against my lips.

I smelled perfume and mystery and adventure. I could hardly remember Jen's name. Let alone my own.

"I'll tell her," I said.

9//the right thing

I picked Jen up for work the next morning. I couldn't tell her about Nicole right before our first day, so I didn't say anything. And at lunch, we took our sandwiches out near the caddy's hut and ate them with a bunch of other kids. So I couldn't do it then. I told myself that I'd tell her as we drove home.

Jen, I'd say, *I've met someone else. It doesn't mean I don't love you. . . .*

Jen, I'd say, *the weirdest thing happened. I met this girl on my computer, and she showed up.*

Jen, I'd say, *do you ever wonder what other guys are like?*

I tried out about a million lines in my head. All of them sounded fake, or mean. And what if Jen cried? I'd crumble as fast as a stale cookie.

"You're so quiet," Jen said on the way home.

"Just thinking about work," I said. "That

restaurant can get really busy. I hope I'm up for it."

"I think you can handle it," Jen said, flashing me a grin. "Just don't drop a tray on the mayor's head."

"Or spill coffee on my dad's boss."

Jen giggled. "Or *your* boss."

We laughed together. I remembered Nicole's lips against mine as she said "Tell her." Just thinking about it made me shiver.

But looking into Jen's trusting eyes and saying "We have to break up" suddenly felt impossible.

Suddenly, the *right* thing felt like the *wrong* thing.

I was in a state of total confusion. So I didn't say anything at all.

Dad made his famous chicken marengo that night. Well, it was famous in the Lanier household. Mostly because once, Dad goofed and used a half jar of cayenne pepper in the sauce. He was the first person to take a bite, and we thought his eyeballs would pop out of his head and go rolling across the floor.

So we have a Lanier family tradition. Dewey and I carefully taste the chicken, then bulge our eyeballs out as far as we can and say, "H-h-h-h-h-h . . ." just like Dad did that memorable night.

Dad laughs every time. Unlike most parentals, he gets a kick out of it when the joke's on him. Usually.

Tonight, I did the old eyeball bulge with Dewey, but my heart wasn't in it. I couldn't stop thinking about Nicole. She was bummed that I had a summer job. She wanted to visit the country club on a day pass, but she promised she wouldn't until I told Jen.

That was all I needed. Nicole sunning herself in a bikini by the pool while Jen stood by with hedge clippers. Ladies and gentlemen, may I present *Mayhem: Part Five*.

"Mom and I have made a decision," Dad said as he spooned some rice onto Annie's plate. "Because of my close encounter with an oak tree, we're going to postpone the European trip until spring break next year. That will give us more time to plan, anyway."

"I already told Timothy I was going!" Dewey said. "He thought it was cool!"

Meanwhile, Annie just went on smashing rice with the tines of her fork. She probably thought Europe was somewhere west of Altoona. Her personal choice for a family vacation is Hershey, Pennsylvania. Her choice is *always* Hershey, Pennsylvania. We've already been there three times.

"We're sorry, Dewey," Mom said. "But your dad really isn't up to touring. We thought instead that we'd go to the cabin a little earlier this year. We didn't rent it out, so it will be empty."

"Can Timmie come?" Dewey asked.

Mom shook her head. "Not this year," she said. "There's not enough room. You know that Jen's coming."

Dewey nodded. Jen is so stellar in his book, he'd sacrifice Timmie for her.

Jen. She'd come to the cabin every year. But this year was different. This year, I had Nicole. How could I handle this one?

"Can you get time off from work next week, Jonah?" Dad asked me.

I nodded. "I can get Toby to cover for me. I'm covering for him when he goes to Cape May in August."

"Why don't you call Jen tonight?" Mom suggested. "She'll have to get time off, too."

"*Mmmm*," I mumbled around a mouthful of chicken and rice.

I would have to invite Jen. But I was seeing Nicole that very night. I remembered telling Matt that meeting Nicole online wouldn't interfere with my life with Jen.

I hated it when Matt turned out to be right.

I picked up Nicole on a street corner in Parson's Ford. Her aunt Mags was "way nosy," according to Nicole, and Nicole didn't want me to be "subjected to her district attorney-like cross-examination."

We went for ice cream, then took our cones to the town green. It was just getting dark, and lights were coming on around the village. Nicole seemed to float against the dusk with her blond hair and pale colors. She dressed in totally cool vintage clothes. Tonight she was wearing this long pale skirt and a pink short-sleeved silk shirt. She wore this close-fitting little straw hat pulled down almost to her eyebrows. Her hair spilled out from underneath it, shining softly in the streetlamps' glow.

We finished our cones, but we stayed on the park bench. Nicole shivered and moved closer. "This is nice."

"Are you cold?"

She nodded, and I slipped my arm around her. She snuggled up next to me. My fingers slid along the silkiness of her shirt. She felt delicate, like she needed protection.

"You didn't tell Jen today, did you," she said.

"I couldn't, somehow."

Nicole slipped her arm around my waist. She hugged me. "It's okay. I understand. It's because you're such a nice guy, Jonah. So loyal. You'll tell her tomorrow, though? Promise?"

"I promise," I said. "The thing is—"

She stiffened. "What thing?"

"Mom and Dad canceled the trip to Europe—"

Nicole snuggled against me again. "Good."

"—And, you see, every year, we go to this cabin up in the Poconos. So we're going to do that again this year, only earlier. And, the thing is—"

She drew away and looked at me. "What thing? What are you trying to tell me, Jonah?"

"Jen has gone with us for the past three years. And, well, Mom told me to ask her this year, too."

Nicole was very still. "And did you?"

"Not yet, but—"

"You *can't*." Nicole's eyes glittered in the light of the streetlamps.

"I don't *want* to," I said. "But—"

Now her eyes filled with tears. "I couldn't bear it, Jonah," she said, her voice breaking. "I couldn't bear thinking of you up in the mountains with her. Can't I go instead? I'm your *real* girlfriend. Can't you ask your parents?"

Jen was so strong. She didn't need me the way Nicole did.

"Can't you ask them, please?" she asked.

"Of course I can," I said.

"Absolutely not," Mom said.

"But, Mom—"

"I already spoke to Jen's mother," Mom said. "Jen is waiting for you to ask her."

"Why do I have to?" I burst out. "Why can't I take who I want?"

Mom pinned me with her eagle eye. "Let me ask you something, Jonah. Have you broken up with Jenny?"

"Well, no," I mumbled.

"So she's still your girlfriend?"

"Well, yes. Technically."

Mom nodded her head a few times. "*Technically*," she repeated. "I see. Well, do you think it's very nice, or very fair, to take another girl to the cabin, if you're still going steady with Jen?"

I was trapped. No question. This was too much for a guy to take. First my best friend had nailed me with the truth, and now my Mom had, too. Mom paused in the doorway of my room. "Jonah," she said in a gentler tone. "You're a teenager, so you probably think my advice is lame."

"Not so!" I said. "I think it's *brilliant*."

Mom grinned. "Sure, kiddo. Well, I'm going to give you some, anyway. You need to do some hard thinking and sort out your feelings. You don't want to throw away a terrific girl like Jen for the sake of someone you don't even know."

"I thought you liked Nicole," I said.

"I don't *know* her," Mom said. "And she doesn't seem like the type of girl you can *get* to know."

"What do you mean?" I asked.

Mom sighed. "I'm not sure. I just want you to be careful, that's all. And I don't want you to hurt Jen."

"I don't want to hurt Jen, either."

"Then don't," Mom said, closing the door.

10//old times

Okay. Things were messed up. I needed to resolve them, pronto.

So I seized the bull by the horns and opted for delay.

Every morning, I drove Jen to work. Every evening, I drove her home. I knew she was waiting for me to ask her to the cabin. Every day, she got quieter and quieter. And I still didn't ask.

Because every night, I saw Nicole. I drove down to Parson's Ford and picked her up at the street corner. Once, we went to the movies, but mostly, we just got ice cream and walked around the quiet streets. Or sat by the river. Or, one rainy night, we just sat in the car, talking.

Every morning, when I picked up Jen, I could hardly look at her. It wasn't just that I felt guilty. It was that my head was full of Nicole.

Finally, one morning, I was running late. I had been talking to Nicole online until two in the morning, and I'd overslept. I saw Jen heading across the front lawn toward the house, and I hurried outside on the porch, still chomping on my bagel.

"Sorry," I said as I tucked in my shirt. "I slept through the alarm."

Jen shaded her eyes with her hand. "No problem. We have time."

Just then, Mom came out on the porch, her car keys in her hand, ready to head off to work.

"Morning, Jen," she said. "Were you able to get time off? I keep forgetting to ask Jonah."

A dead silence fell. Jen blushed and looked away. Luckily, my mouth was full of bagel so I couldn't say anything.

Mom looked from Jen to me. She frowned. "Jonah? Didn't you ask Jen to the cabin yet?"

The bagel felt like a mouthful of cotton. I swallowed, hard. "Um, I haven't had a chance."

Mom didn't bother pointing out that I'd been driving back and forth to work with Jen all week long. She just raised an eyebrow at me.

"Jen, can you get next week off?" I asked.

It had never occurred to me before, but maybe waiting this long was a good strategy. Maybe Jen wouldn't be able to swing time off. We'd just started working, after all.

Okay. It hadn't been strategy. It had been

cowardice. But at this point, I'd take what I could get.

"I think so," Jen said. "My boss knows that we all take family vacations. I'd just have to switch with someone."

Oh, well. So much for that strategy.

Jen broke into a smile. "I'm sure I can make it," she said.

"Almost there," Dad said.

"Ten miles to the turnoff," Dewey sang out.

Jen looked out the window.

It had been a long, uncomfortable ride out to the cottage. Here's the trouble with being really close to your girlfriend: You pretty much always know what she is thinking. Jen was wondering why I'd been so distant. Why I waited so long to ask her to the cottage. Why I'd been so quiet on our drives to work. Why we never did anything at night anymore. Why I didn't call her at seven-thirty every night. Why I hadn't invited her to Friday night dinner in two weeks.

And she was wondering if I wanted her on this family trip at all.

I wanted to squeeze her hand, or give her a look to let her know that everything was okay. But everything *wasn't* okay. As Nicole said, if I acted the same with Jen, I'd just be leading her on.

Nicole. She'd gone all white and still when I'd told her that Mom had forced me to invite Jen. So I'd just kept on talking. I'd tried to make Nicole feel better by telling her about how important tradition was to my family.

We have this whole routine, I'd explained. We even have this certain order that we do things in when we get to the cottage.

First, we unload the car. But we don't unpack even one suitcase—we just put all the bags in the bedrooms and the food in the kitchen. Then we all walk down to the lake. We take off our shoes and just stand there, letting the water wash over our toes, and check out the boats and the marshy grass, and the state of the dock and canoes.

Then we go back up to the cottage. Dad wrestles the grill out from the aluminum shed and sets it up. Mom takes Annie over to our next-door neighbors, the MacFarlands, to say hello. Dewey and I set up the badminton set. And Jen puts away the food and makes a big pitcher of iced tea, with plenty of lemon and mint.

If I thought explaining how Jen was part of the routine would make Nicole feel better, I was about a million miles off base. Her face had just gotten sadder and sadder.

"It sounds like so much fun," she'd said wistfully.

My heart had cracked open, right then and there. All I'd wished for at that moment was that Nicole was coming with us instead of Jen.

And maybe Jen sensed that. Maybe that's why she looked so lost today.

"Turn off!" Dad cried.

"Turn off!" Annie echoed. She was such a goofball. She has the only red hair in the family, and sometimes I call her the Recessive Gene. But only if Mom isn't around.

Annie only liked to wear red and orange clothes. "Because they match," she'd say matter-of-factly. Today, she was dressed in a stunning outfit of red shorts and an orange T-shirt.

"I sure hope Jonah doesn't fall out of the canoe again this year," Dad said.

"Hey," I said. "I didn't *fall* out."

Dewey snorted. "You didn't *dive* out."

"What I mean is," I said, "it wasn't my fault. Jen was rocking the canoe."

"Me?" Jen said. "It was you! You were trailing your hand in the water, and you thought a snake bit you, even though it was just a big old branch—"

"It *looked* like a snake—"

"So you jumped up," Jen continued, "and you tripped over my paddle—"

"I was actually trying to steady the canoe so that *you* wouldn't tip it over," I pointed out.

Jen smirked. "What, by screaming, 'Snake! Snake!'?"

"No," I said. "By falling in."

Everyone burst out laughing.

"Well, it didn't work," Jen said, laughing. "Because I fell in, too."

She grinned at me, and I grinned back. And suddenly, everything was okay again. The funny thing is, when your girlfriend is your best friend, it makes things easy.

And it makes things hard.

Suddenly, Jen's eyes twinkled. "Uh-oh," she said to me. "I'm sensing something. Could it be . . ."

"I think it might . . .," I said.

Annie giggled. She knew what was coming.

"It's nerd alert!" Jen and I shouted together.

Annie squealed as Jen dropped a beach towel over her head. I held on to the ends, and Jen tickled Annie. We'd been doing this to the poor kid since she was two years old. We throw whatever's handy over her head and then tickle her until she begs for mercy.

You have to pick your moment, though. We

usually waited until the cottage was in sight. One summer, we'd pulled a "nerd alert" in the middle of the trip, and Annie had thrown up her cheese snack all over Mom's antique quilt.

"Okay, kids, that's enough torture," Dad said. "We're here!"

The routine began. We unloaded the car. We looked at the lake and got our feet wet. Mom went off down the trail with Annie. Dad cleaned off the grill. Jen disappeared into the cottage, and Dewey and I started to untangle the net. Everything had to be set up in time for the traditional before-dinner badminton match.

A few minutes later, Jen stuck her head out of the screen door just as Dewey started banging on a spike. Her lips were moving, but I couldn't make out what she was saying. I motioned her over.

Jen jumped down the porch stairs and bounded toward me.

"I can't find the lemons," she called, smiling. "Do you—"

But she didn't finish her sentence. Because just then, the cottage blew up.

11//smithereens

The impact of the explosion sent Jen to her knees. I ran toward her, feeling the heat against my face.

"Jen! Are you okay?"

Her eyes were wide and frightened. "What happened?"

I helped her up. Dad hurried toward us from the side of the house. And then I saw Mom running from the direction of the MacFarlands', her face panicked. I saw her eyes move from Dad to Dewey to me to Jen. Relief crossed her face, but her pace didn't slacken. Behind her, Mrs. MacFarland was running hand in hand with Annie.

We all stood in a row. Shocked, scared, glad to be alive. And we watched the cottage burn.

"Gas leak," the fire chief said. "Happens all the time with these summer places."

"But everything was checked out last

month," Dad said. "I hired someone to inspect everything—wiring, roof, gas."

He shrugged. "Well, somebody messed up, then. I've seen it before. Maybe the guy has a dozen places to check, and he gets sloppy. It happens."

"I've been coming here for twenty years," my dad said slowly. "Since I was a kid. My kids grew up here. A piece of history is gone."

"Yeah." The fireman looked at the black, smoking wood. "It hap—," he started. Then he looked at the distress on my dad's face, and my mom's, and at all of us kids.

"I'm sorry about your place," he said.

It was a long, depressing ride home. Dad and Mom didn't say much. Mom halfheartedly said that they'd think of another fun vacation. But nobody said what we all were thinking—that so far, their track record wasn't great.

The whole thing felt strange. It was like Dad said: A piece of history was gone. So many summers with Jen, wiped out in an instant. It was like our past together was wiped out, too.

Jen went home, and we carried what little we were able to salvage back inside. Mom and Dad lingered on the porch. I drifted close to a window to listen.

"Maybe I sound superstitious," Mom said.

"But you know they say that disasters come in threes."

"Come here," Dad said. He hugged her, and they rocked together for a minute, Mom's head against his shoulder.

"I can't help it," Mom said, so softly that I could barely hear her. "But I keep wondering, what's next?"

Nicole left me an e-mail saying she was sorry she'd been so upset about Jen going to the cottage.

I hope you have a fantastic time, she wrote. *Of course, I'll miss you like crazy.*

I was too beat to answer her that night. And I was too rushed the next morning. She wouldn't be expecting to hear from me, anyway, since she thought I was still in the mountains.

Jen and I decided to go to work. We called in, and we both got shifts. It felt good to wipe down tables and lift trays and keep running all morning. I could forget about the sudden shock of the noise and flames and the way Jen had fallen, as if the explosion had blown her down.

It was getting close to lunchtime when I heard Toby, another busboy, whistle under his breath. "Pinch me, Lanier," he said.

"Gladly," I said. "Why?"

"Because I've got to be dreaming," he said. "Girls don't look like that in Milleridge, Pennsylvania."

I turned. Nicole stood at the hostess desk. She was dressed in this fifties-style pink suit, only with a short skirt. She wore black patent leather heels, and a pink headband swept back her golden hair. She was even wearing short white gloves. She looked great.

She waved when she saw me. "Jonah!"

"You know her?" Toby breathed. "Can I, like, touch you?"

Nicole walked toward me. "I heard about the cottage," she said. "I feel terrible. I was supposed to have lunch in Philadelphia with my aunt, but I canceled it. I just had to see you."

"Uh, thanks for coming, Nicole," I said. "How did you find out?"

"I was in Milleridge doing some shopping and I saw your mom and Annie," Nicole explained, her blue eyes dark with worry. "I just had to see for myself that you were okay."

"I'm okay," I said. "Nicole, I can't really talk. I'm working—"

"I know," she said. "I won't get you in trouble. I just had to . . . oh, Jonah!"

Suddenly, Nicole threw her arms around me.

"I'm so glad you're safe," she murmured, pressing herself against me.

I don't want to say that it didn't feel good. But I was in the middle of work, and it was kind of embarrassing. All the busboys and waiters were staring, and my boss, Andy Hollister, looked ticked off.

But that was nothing compared to what happened when Jen walked in.

12//ooo-la-la

I saw her over Nicole's shoulder. I saw how the smile on her face grew puzzled. I saw how the image of another girl with her arms around me slowly trickled in.

Nicole must have noticed that I'd turned into a piece of wood. Slowly, her arms slipped down. She turned and saw Jen.

I saw recognition flash in Jen's eyes, and I knew she remembered the picture in my wallet. For a minute, I thought she would turn and run. But Jen never runs away from anything. She approached us, slapping her work gloves in her palm. Her face was flushed an angry pink.

"Hello, Jen," Nicole said quietly. "I'm sorry you had to find out this way."

"Do I *know* you?" Jen flung at Nicole.

It seemed like the time for even a coward like me to step in, so I did. "Jen. This is—"

"Nicole," Nicole said softly.

"Your *French* cousin. Well, *ooo-la-la*," Jen

said bitterly. "She doesn't have much of a French accent, Jonah."

"Jen—"

"Save it!" Jen snapped. "Just save it, Jonah." Her eyes filled with tears. "You pig," she said, her voice breaking. She turned and ran out of the restaurant.

Okay, I was a pig. I'm not denying it. But I was a pig with a heart.

I couldn't let Jen go like that. Maybe if I explained, it would help. Maybe if I told her how the thing with Nicole had snowballed, she'd begin to see. I knew that no matter how angry Jen was, the hurt was the worst part. I couldn't let her think that I didn't still care about her.

I had a feeling that my explanation wouldn't go over like butter. But it would be better than my staying here with Nicole.

I took a step toward the exit, but Nicole put her hand on my arm.

"Let her go, Jonah," Nicole said softly. "I know it's hard. But you'll just make her feel worse. There really isn't anything you can say to make her feel better about this. Is there?"

"I don't know," I said. "I can't let her leave like that!"

"Well, I know girls," Nicole said. "And she's

in no state to listen right now."

"Yeah," I said. "I guess."

"What's done is done," Nicole said. "She had to find out. It's finally over."

"Yeah," I said. I'd seen the look on Jen's face. Nicole was right. "It is."

I had wanted a different life that summer. Well, I'd gotten it. I'd griped that I saw too much of Jen. Well, now I never saw her at all.

Jen disappeared. Her mom drove her to work every morning before I'd even had breakfast. She must have waited until I left the club before she took off. Because I never saw her. Every window shade in her house was pulled down on the side facing our house.

Meanwhile, Nicole suddenly got very . . . visible. Every day after work, she waited for me outside the gates of the country club.

Even though Jen didn't see her, all the other kids who worked there did. Tell me I'm wrong, but I think the news got back to her.

And Nicole liked to sit in my backyard after work. We'd make some lemonade, or grab some sodas, and sit on the grass. The only trouble was, the spot is perfectly visible from the back windows of Jen's house. Nicole didn't realize that. But it made me feel terrible.

But how could I say, *Nicole, would you mind sitting inside on this gorgeous summer day because my ex-girlfriend might see you?*

Even I wasn't that much of a jerk.

I got to know Nicole better. Or actually, she got to know *me* better. Unlike most gorgeous girls, she didn't like to talk about herself. I guess it was because of her parents dying in that terrible accident. It was like she had these really deep wounds that she didn't want to expose to the air. Her eyes would turn that dark blue, and she'd tilt her chin down, and she'd go all quiet and still.

And that made me want to protect her all the more.

So I didn't push when Nicole told me that she didn't want me to meet her aunt Mags. At first, she tried to laugh it off.

"She'd trap you in her kitchen and feed you her awful oatmeal cookies," Nicole said. "I'd be mortified."

"So I'll just nibble on one," I said. "How bad can it be?"

"The thing is, Jonah," Nicole said hesitantly, "Aunt Mags is my mom's sister. She never got over my parents' death. She's really bitter and unhappy, and she wants me to stay that way, too."

"What do you mean?" I asked, puzzled.

Nicole looked down and ran her fingertip along my wrist. We were in the backyard after work, sitting in the shade of the big maple. Her long eyelashes cast bluish shadows on her cheeks.

"Well, she's still mourning my mom, and she wants company," Nicole said. "So every time I seem happy, or I laugh, she . . . goes crazy. She tells me I'm forgetting my mom. But I'm not!" Nicole's eyes were full of tears. "I miss my mom, every day. But I can't help it if I want to be happy! Is that so bad of me, Jonah?"

I was shocked. How could an adult be so mean? "Of course you're not bad!" I said. "Your aunt is so wrong, Nicole. She shouldn't put that kind of trip on you. She needs a shrink."

"The thing is, if you came over," Nicole said, "and she saw that I had a boyfriend, she'd make me pay after you were gone. It would just be easier if you'd stay away. Would you do that for me?" she asked pleadingly.

I slipped my arms around her. "Of course I will," I said. Just when I thought she was the golden girl, she turned around and showed me that, compared to everyone I knew, Nicole had it tough. But she never complained about it.

How could you not be crazy about a girl like that?

I went in to the kitchen to get more sodas. Mom was sitting at the table, husking corn.

"Is Nicole staying for dinner again?" she asked, her eyes on the corn.

I closed the refrigerator door. "I guess. Is that okay?"

Mom didn't answer for a minute. She peeled off a strand of corn silk and dropped the husked corn in the pot.

"Mom? I thought you liked Nicole."

"She's a very nice girl," Mom said.

But I was wise to parental code. I knew that what Mom really meant was, *What's my baby boy doing with that witch?*

"I don't get it," I said. "Nicole is superhelpful around the house. She always washes the dishes, or offers to, and she talks to Dad about his gardening ideas for hours, and plays catch with Dewey. She even told Annie she has a great sense of color."

"Exactly," Mom said. "The girl works very hard."

The soda cans felt cold, and I put them down on the kitchen table. "You're always telling me to be fair when it comes to other people. I don't think you're being very fair to Nicole. Just because you like Jen—"

"This isn't about Jenny." Mom put down the half-husked ear of corn and turned to me. "I don't know, Jonah. Maybe I *am* being unfair. But there's something about Nicole . . . she's never spontaneous. I've never heard her laugh too hard or say the wrong thing or be shy or . . . oh, I don't know. Everything she does seems so . . . studied."

"She wants you to like her," I said.

Mom nodded. "I know. But do I have to like her every single day? She never leaves you alone, Jonah. At least you and Jen had separate interests."

"She's lonely," I said. "You know she has no family. And it can't be easy coming here when she knows Jen was practically a member of the family."

"I realize that," Mom said. "It's not that I want her to feel uncomfortable. But a little self-consciousness would go a long way with me. That girl just breezes into this house as though she belongs here. She seems completely comfortable taking Jen's place. Like it was really hers all along. Nicole is always so . . . *composed*."

"What are you saying, Mom? I finally get a girl with poise, so I should dump her?"

Mom wound corn silk around her finger. "That's not what I'm saying."

"Should I tell her not to come to dinner anymore?"

Mom picked up the ear and began to shuck it again. "No, of course not. It's just that—"

We both heard the screen door open and shut. Nicole appeared, smiling. "Mrs. Lanier! Jonah and I can do that!"

Mom waved the ear of corn. "That's okay, Nicole. Actually, I enjoy shucking—"

"I insist." Smiling brightly, Nicole snatched the ear out of Mom's hand. She swiped the bowl of unshucked corn off the table. Then she nodded her chin toward the pot. "Come on, Jonah. Let's take these outside."

She marched out of the kitchen while Mom stared after her, openmouthed. The screen door banged.

Mom looked across the kitchen at me. I shrugged. So Nicole took domestic chores seriously. She just wanted to be helpful.

"Jonah—," Mom began softly.

But Nicole stuck her head in the screen door. "Jonah? You coming?"

I picked up the corn pot. I didn't meet Mom's eyes. "I'm coming," I said.

After dinner, Nicole and I had planned to walk along the river, but the rain started during dessert, and we canceled the plan. Instead, we turned on my computer to play double solitaire.

I beat Nicole twice. She didn't have the best concentration.

"Okay," I said. "This is the championship match. Whoever wins will be ruler of the world."

"Loser goes first," Nicole said, turning the computer screen toward her. Just then, my e-mail flag popped up.

I reached over and clicked on my mailbox, just to see who it was from.

"ToddWan4," I said. "I don't know who that is."

"Probably just junk mail," Nicole said. "I get it all the time. Hey, it's my turn." She swung the computer back and clicked, and the e-mail disappeared.

"Nicole! You just trashed my mail!" I said.

Her hand flew to her mouth. "Oh, my gosh! Your program is different from mine. Jonah, I'm sorry! I thought I was just saving it for later!"

"It's okay," I said. "If it's important, they'll mail me again. I don't know who ToddWan4 is, anyway."

Nicole clicked back into the game. "I've never told you this, but my secret ambition is to be ruler of the world. So your mom had better watch out."

Her eyes gleamed at me. There was something in her smile that made a shiver run up my spine. It was mid-July, so it couldn't have been from the wind whistling through the cracks of the house. And it couldn't have been that for a moment, I'd caught a glimpse of something dark and scary in my dream girl.

It must have been the air-conditioning.

13//river's edge

Something about the shades pulled down on Jen's house gave me the creeps. And never seeing her was weird. It was like the person that was so there all the time—like Dewey or Annie—was just a blank spot suddenly.

I really needed to get away from the shadow of the Malone house. The old house even seemed to lean now, tilting toward our house as if it would fall, *splat*, and annihilate us.

It was time for a road trip.

I picked up Nicole at the town green. She wasn't hard to spot. All I had to do was follow the gaze of every guy between nine and ninety.

I usually don't notice girls' clothes, but I always was struck with what Nicole wore. Today, she was dressed in a floaty white dress, and sandals with straps that crisscrossed around her ankles. She wore a straw hat with a big red flower on the brim, and short net gloves. If the outfit sounds weird, it wasn't. She looked fantastic.

But let's face it, Nicole could wear a paper sack and look like she belonged on a magazine cover.

I had borrowed my mom's basket and plates and things, but Nicole had insisted on buying all the food for our picnic. She'd brought all my favorites. Barbecue potato chips. Turkey and Swiss cheese sandwiches with hot mustard. Sweet pickles. Herring in sour cream. French-fried onion rings. Green apples. Those hot Italian peppers stuffed with cheese. Tortilla chips and salsa. She would have packed those little frozen pizza rolls if she could have dragged along a freezer and a microwave.

"Who else is coming?" I asked, looking at all the food. "The Fourth Battalion?"

"I just want you to be happy," Nicole said.

I headed upriver to the park. Here, the river widened. There were bluffs that rose high along the riverbank, and you could see rapids out in the middle of the river. It looked like a wild and lonely spot, but actually, the main road was just a few yards away. Still, there were plenty of secluded places for a picnic.

We spread out the blanket close enough to see the river but far enough away so that the grass wasn't damp.

I didn't want to hurt Nicole's feelings, so I ate a little of everything. And way too many stuffed peppers and cheese. Then Nicole sliced up the apples, and we chomped away.

"Oof," I said, lying back. "I feel like a tick on a hound dog."

"How about dessert? I brought pecan cookies."

"Can't," I said. "I'm allergic to nuts. I'll swell up like a float in the Macy's Thanksgiving Day parade. Besides, I can't eat another bite."

Nicole tugged at my hand. "I know the cure for that. You need to burn off some calories."

I sat up again. "Let's go for a swim."

Nicole's smile dimmed. "I . . . can't swim, Jonah."

"You can't swim?" I asked, incredulous. I'd never heard of anyone who couldn't swim. I'd grown up by a river, and I'd been swimming practically before I'd been walking.

"I never learned," Nicole confessed. She twisted her gloved hands. "When my parents' plane got hit, it skidded off the runway into the bay," she said in a voice so soft, I had to bend over to hear. "They drowned, still strapped to their seats. Ever since then . . ."

I squeezed her hand in sympathy. "Let's go for a walk, then."

She lifted her head and gave me a knockout smile. It made my heart feel like it had just been squashed flat at a Monster Truck Rally.

Hand in hand, we climbed up the grassy bank toward the woods. Jen and I used to walk here if we needed some peace. We'd come here a lot during that summer when her brother was in rehab.

Stop thinking about Jen, I told myself.

But it suddenly got hard *not* to think about Jen. Because she was right in front of me.

She was dressed in cutoffs and a baseball cap, and she was swinging a baseball glove. Matt was with her, and Tommy, and the rest of the crowd from school.

Then I remembered. Every summer, the third Friday in July, we had a guys-against-the-girls softball game. The guys had called it "Bulls versus Heifers," but somehow the name never caught on with the girls.

I saw Matt lean over to tell Jen something. Jen shut her eyes and tilted her head back for a second before letting go with a big laugh. She only laughs like that if something is really funny. What could Matt have said that was so hysterical? He isn't that funny. I dropped Nicole's hand.

"It's your friends," Nicole said. "They haven't seen you yet. We can go back to the river—"

"Jonesey! Jones Boy! Jone-o-Mat!" Tommy Brandon caught sight of me. "You showed!"

"We have our first baseman," Jeremy said.

Jen's face flushed. She looked down and fiddled with her glove. Matt glanced at her and looked back at me, his eyes flat.

"It doesn't look to me like Jonah came to play," Matt said.

"I forgot there was a game," I said.

"Well, there's a game," Tommy said impatiently. "Are you in?"

"I have an extra glove," Jeremy said.

I knew that Nicole wanted to go back to our picnic. I knew that she wanted to be alone with me.

But we were *always* alone. I never saw my friends anymore. I'd been so wrapped up in the fact that I never saw Jen that I didn't realize that I hadn't seen Matt in weeks. It was even kind of nice to see Tommy Brandon. When that happened, you knew you'd been alone too long.

"Sure," I said. "I'll play."

"All *right*!" Jeremy said.

I turned to Nicole. "Is this okay? It's kind of a tradition. The guys play against the girls, and afterward we all go for a swim."

Nicole nodded. "Of course it's okay. I'd adore watching you play."

We all headed for the diamond. Ahead of us,

the rest of the girls moved to surround Jen, as if Nicole would attack her or something. A few of them gave me looks they might give to a serial killer. Obviously, the word was out. I was a slimeball weevil.

In the history of the guys-against-the-girls game, this one would break all records for errors and downright bonehead moves. Balls were dropped, bases were completely missed, and Greg Villanova got beaned with a high fly.

There's no telling what devastation an out-of-town babe can spread. All the guys were keeping one eye on the ball and one eye on Nicole, and it showed.

I was torn. On the one hand, seeing the hurt in Jen's eyes—or rather, *imagining* it, since she kept her baseball cap tugged down low—was my idea of extreme torture. On the other hand, it was way past cool to have the other guys get their toes smashed and noggins conked, just for ogling *my* girlfriend.

Nicole sat on the top seat of the bleachers, her feet on the row below. She waved at me whenever I looked over. All the other onlookers—mostly girls—sat about a mile away from her. They made this big effort not to look at her. During the fifth inning, when Tommy

Brandon was on deck, he sauntered over to me. He put his big foot on the bench next to me and leaned over. "I admire your taste, man," he said, jerking his chin toward Nicole on the bleachers.

I couldn't resist. "Pretty good for a cyber nightmare, huh, Tommy?"

But Jeremy hit a double, and Tommy was next at bat. He hurried to home plate, probably with relief, since he would have had to massively strain his brain to come up with a snappy comeback.

Jen was playing second base. She was a fantastic softball player, but she was off her game that day. She had bobbled the return throw on Jeremy's double, and he had advanced to third.

"Baloney Malone-y," Tommy yelled toward the field. "Your playing stinks today."

Jen tilted the brim of her hat. "Just following your example, Brandon," she called back. "How about a rope swing contest after the game?"

"I'm there, baby!" Tommy yelled back. He was such an idiot. Then, with a glance toward Nicole, he started to knock his bat against his cleats. Only he wasn't wearing cleats, so he smashed himself in the ankle.

Jen sat out two innings. Then she came back and she was in the zone. She even hit a home run in the bottom of the eighth.

The bleachers exploded in cheers, and I looked over to see how Nicole was taking it. But her seat was empty.

It stayed empty during the ninth inning—which was a drag, because I played brilliantly, socking a solid triple when our team was up. Then, I made the stunning diving catch that ended the game. We barely squeaked by the girls, 7–6.

When I looked over at the bleachers, Nicole was there, applauding like crazy. She blew me a kiss.

Jen saw it. I thought I knew all her expressions, but I'd never seen this one. Her face just sort of crumpled with hurt. Then she bit her lower lip and frowned and rubbed her glove, like there was a really horrible stain on it. I felt like my heart was an accordion. *Squeeeeze . . . wail . . . squeeeeze.*

Matt walked past me toward the bleachers. "I can't believe you brought that girl here," he said furiously. "Are you out of your mind, or just really mean?"

"Her name is Nicole," I said.

"Don't you know what this is doing to Jen?" Matt's face was dark red. And it wasn't from sunburn.

Tell me I'm wrong. But when it comes to

teenagers, we *always* have to argue. Especially when your best friend accuses you of something, and he's right on the money.

So even though I wanted to tell Matt that I'd forgotten about the game, and I never would have brought Nicole here if I'd known, I hit back. "Since when is protecting Jen your business?" I snapped.

"I never knew what a lame jerk you were, Lanier," Matt said disgustedly. He stomped off.

I wanted to slug Matt. Probably because he was right. Even though I hadn't meant to push Nicole in Jen's face, the truth was that I had.

I walked by the benches, where Jen was now knocking the dust off her athletic shoes.

"Great homer," I said.

She didn't look up. She didn't say a word. Not *Thanks*, or *Yeah, my bat was hot today*, or even, *Get lost, jerk*.

I just stood there. I couldn't believe Jen, my Jen, could freeze me out that way.

Then she looked up. Her eyes were cool, and they looked right past me.

"Hey, Brandon," she called. "You up for that swinging contest? Or are you hoping I'll forget?"

Tommy yelled back. "Me Tarzan!"

Jen flashed a grin. "Me Jane!"

Tommy gave his version of a yodel, and everyone started motoring toward the river.

I slowly headed for Nicole. I felt hot, and tired, and angry, and I didn't know who I was angry at. Matt? Jen? Tommy? Myself?

"Awesome catch," Nicole said, jumping down the bleachers toward me.

"I need a swim," I said.

We followed the other kids to the river. Every summer, some kids tied a rope swing on top of the bluff. Usually, some park ranger type guy untied it, since adults thought it was dangerous. But someone else always went right back and tied another hank of rope up there.

True to their nature, adults were worrying too much. It wasn't really that dangerous to swing off the bluff. I'd done it plenty of times, and I wasn't the bravest dude in the world. First of all, it wasn't that high. Only about twenty feet. And the river was way deep in that spot. The one danger was, if you didn't swing out far enough, you could fall on the rocks by the shore.

"I'm first, Tarzan," Jen called to Tommy. "I'll stay where I land, and you see if you can swing out farther."

"What do I get when I do?" Tommy asked, smirking.

"I'll think about it," Jen said.

Everyone yelled out, "*Whoaaaaaa.*"

Nicole drifted closer to me. "Poor Jen," she said. "She'll do anything to get your attention."

"Nicole, *shhh*," I said. But I knew her voice had carried, and Jen had heard.

Jen's chin set. She took off up the steep slope of the bluff like a jackrabbit.

"I'll stay here," Nicole told me softly.

I climbed up the bluff after the other kids. By the time we reached the top, Jen was standing with the rope in her hand. She backed up as far as she could to give herself a running start. She would have to let go at the highest point of the rope's arc so that she would fall into the deep part of the river.

Jen ran, her tanned legs flashing. She leaped off the cliff and swung out over the river. But something was wrong. I heard a *snap*, and the rope broke. Jen screamed. And then she plummeted straight down to the rocks below!

14//accusations

It all happened so fast. I didn't even have time to panic. I saw Jen in the air, her arms and legs pumping, as though she could get traction in the air, enough to clear the rocks.

Then she was out of sight. We heard the splash of Jen landing as we ran toward the edge of the bluff.

A funny thing happened to me: Time slowed down. It seemed to take forever for me to reach the edge of the bluff, even though I was running. It was like I was moving through marshmallow goo. I let out a cry of relief when I saw Jen's head, dark as a seal, surface beyond the rocks.

Barely beyond the rocks.

Then I noticed that she was treading water with one hand. Her voice was faint, but I heard her call.

"What?" I shouted.

"She's hurt," Matt said. He turned and took off down the bluff.

I wanted to leap off the bluff right there and save her. But I'd just end up smashed on the rocks. And some swimmers in the shallow water were already stroking toward Jen. She started to swim to meet them, using one arm. Her face was just a white blur from where I was, so I couldn't tell if she was in a lot of pain.

I took off after Matt. At the bottom of the bluff, I almost ran into Nicole. Her face was perfectly blank. Then it contracted into an expression of concern.

"Is she okay?"

"I don't know," I said. I ran past her and half-slid, half-ran toward the bank.

Jen sat, cradling her arm. Kids gathered around her, and Matt draped somebody's denim vest over her shoulders, which wasn't very helpful, since it kept slipping off. Matt just kept putting it back on again.

"I'm okay, really," Jen said. She was shaking. "But I think I might have sprained my wrist."

"It could be broken," Matt said. "I'll drive you to the hospital."

"I wish everyone would stop fussing," Jen said. She tried to smile, but it looked like a wince.

That's how she was. She hated to be fussed over. But even though Matt kept trying to cover her with a little denim vest like a lamebrain, I wished I were there, doing the same thing.

"I'll go get the car and bring it around," Matt said. But he didn't move. He crouched in front of Jen, anxiously staring into her face.

Then Jen's gaze traveled past Matt's shoulder, past me, and locked on something behind me.

Some*one*. Nicole.

Nicole had the same expression on her face as before. Everyone else looked shocked, and scared, and confused. Nicole just looked . . . blank. It was like nothing bad had happened at all. She could have been admiring the river, or waiting for a bus.

Nicole is always so composed, Mom had said. *A little self-consciousness would go a long way with me.*

"It was her," Jen said. "She did it!"

Shock rippled through all of us, taking us by surprise.

"What do you mean?" Matt asked her.

"She cut the rope," Jen said. She was shivering badly now, and Matt draped the denim vest over her again. This time, he held it there.

I looked over at Nicole. Her dark blue eyes were full of shock as she stared at Jen.

"Nicole wasn't anywhere near you," I said to Jen.

"She could have been near the *rope*," Jen shot back. "During the game."

"That rope is old," I said. "Somebody should have replaced it this summer."

"Somebody did," Tommy Brandon said. "Me."

"Well, you didn't tie it tightly enough," I said.

Nicole still hadn't said a word. She just stood there. The wind caught her hair and blew it back behind her shoulders. Her dress flowed out behind her like a train.

Tommy darted behind her and ran up the slope.

A few moments later, he appeared above our heads. He held the rope in his hand.

"Jen is right," he said. "This rope has been cut."

Jen turned to Nicole. "You disappeared during the game. Where were you?" Jen's voice was sharp. It cut through the humid air like a flashing knife.

Nicole had a pained expression on her face when she looked at Jen. "I was with Matt."

"Hah!" Jen spat out.

Everyone looked at Matt.

"It's true," he mumbled. "By the water fountain."

Jen gave Matt an incredulous look. "You were talking to Nicole?"

He lifted one shoulder. "She started talking to me. I couldn't just walk away."

"And then he walked me back to the bleachers," Nicole said. "I wasn't out of his sight."

"It's true, Jen," Matt said reluctantly.

Nicole's blue eyes were wide with concern. "I'm sorry you fell, Jen. And I know you must be in shock. But it wasn't my fault."

Jen didn't say anything. Her lips pressed together, draining them of any color they had. She leaned against Matt's shoulder.

"We've got to get you to a doctor," Matt said.

I couldn't believe Jen could accuse Nicole of such a thing. But Jen knew that Matt wouldn't lie. While Matt helped Jen up and toward the car, I went to stand next to Nicole.

"Sorry about that," I said. "She's just upset."

"I know," Nicole said. She slipped her hand into mine. Her fingers were cool as they entwined with mine. "Let's go home."

Nicole didn't say anything on the drive back. I didn't, either. I was too busy worrying about Jen.

It had been a close call. And what if her wrist

was broken? She'd probably lose her job. And she wouldn't be able to play tennis or swim all summer. Jen would hate that.

I guess I was kind of ignoring Nicole. As a matter-of-fact, I sort of forgot she was even in the car.

"Do you want a cookie?" she asked. "There's plenty left."

"I told you, I'll turn into a float," I said.

"Huh?"

"I'm allergic to nuts, remember?" I snapped.

Then I heard a little *sniff*. I looked over and saw a tear glazing the curve of Nicole's cheek.

"It's not that bad," I said. "I can eat pistachios." Nicole didn't smile. "Are you okay?" I asked. "I didn't mean to snap at you."

"I just feel so awful, Jonah. It's such a horrible thing to be accused of. But the funny thing is, I really don't blame Jen."

"You don't?"

Nicole turned her tear-filled eyes to me. "How could I? She lost you. No wonder she went crazy."

"She didn't go *crazy*," I said. "She was just in shock."

"Right," Nicole said. "I'm sure that was it."

I bypassed the Milleridge turn and headed for Parson's Ford.

"You're taking me home?" Nicole asked.

"I'm really beat, Nicole," I said. "I just want to crash after dinner. I'll see you tomorrow, okay?"

"Okay," Nicole said faintly.

When we got to the green, Nicole leaned over and kissed me on the cheek, then slid out of the car.

I waved and took off. Something was nagging at me. It was probably just worry about Jen. Could I call the Malones and find out how she was? Mrs. Malone would probably hang up on me. Maybe I could call Matt. He'd probably hang up on me, too.

I stomped into the house, carrying the picnic basket. I unpacked it and washed our plastic plates and glasses. I threw away the half-eaten food and saved the rest.

Nicole had seemed really upset, I thought; maybe I should call her tonight. On the bank, after Jen had accused her, she'd been shaking, too. When I held her hand, her fingers had felt so cold. . . .

Her fingers . . .

Her gloves.

Nicole hadn't been wearing those net gloves at the end of the day. She could have put them in her purse, I supposed. But she hadn't carried a purse today.

The picnic basket was empty. I upended it over the garbage pail, shaking the crumbs out over the garbage. The half-eaten apple cores tumbled out.

Wait a sec. The dishes were stacked in the drainer. Two plates, two glasses, two forks.

But where was my paring knife?

15//suspicion

It wasn't that I suspected Nicole, exactly. And I didn't know how she could have cut the rope, if she'd been in sight all afternoon. She'd never even been up on the bluff.

But I just wanted to be sure. The funny thing was, it wasn't that her gloves were missing, or even that I couldn't find the knife.

It was that blank expression on her face. I'd felt the same shiver I'd felt when she'd said, *My secret ambition is to be ruler of the world. So your mom had better watch out.*

I had to wait until after dinner to drive back to the river. Dusk was gathering as I parked the car and hurried up the steep path of the bluff. At the top, I swept my flashlight along the ground.

I was looking for the glint of a knife, or the gleam of her white gloves. I didn't expect to find them. I didn't *want* to find them.

It was so dark here, and lonely. I had to strain to hear the occasional whisper of car tires on the road nearby. But I could hear the river, murmuring over the rocks.

And then I heard something else—footsteps. Coming up the path, toward the top of the bluff. I switched off my flashlight and faded back into the brush.

My heart pounded as the footsteps grew closer. I could see a flashlight bobbing up the trail. I could just make out a dark figure.

The flashlight swept the area near the rope swing. Something about the way the figure moved was familiar. I stepped out to get a closer look, and a twig snapped. The flashlight swung toward me and shone full in my face.

"Hey!" I cried, shielding my eyes.

"Jonah!" The flashlight switched off. It was Jen. "What are you doing here?"

I walked toward her, my eyes still blinking from the harsh light. "Tommy said the rope was cut. I thought maybe somebody left a clue."

Jen looked at me shrewdly. "Someone like Nicole?"

"No . . ."

"You believe me!" Jen cried.

"No," I said firmly, shaking my head. "Nicole wouldn't do something like that. There's got to be another explanation."

A voice came from behind me. "How touching," Matt said sarcastically. "I think I'm gonna cry. Lend me your hankie, Jen."

"What are you doing here?" I asked Matt irritably. Was he glued to Jen's side?

Matt turned to Jen. "Did you find anything?"

"There's nothing up here," I said.

Jen gave me a scornful look, then switched back on her flashlight. I noticed now that her wrist was bound with an Ace bandage. That meant it was a sprain, not a break. Good.

I waited while Jen and Matt searched every inch of the bluff, covering the same ground that I had. Nothing.

"You see?" I said.

"It doesn't mean she didn't do it," Jen said stubbornly. "I just know it was her."

"Jen, if there's no evidence, it's not fair of you to accuse Nicole," I said. "She was really upset after we left."

"Whoa, I'm so sorry," Jen said sardonically. "Matt, can I have my hankie back?"

"I don't trust her, either," Matt said. "Come on, Jonah, don't you think there's something strange about the girl? You should have heard her quizzing me by the water fountain today. She asked about a million questions about you and your family. Don't you think that's weird?

And have you noticed that you've completely dropped out of sight to be with her? That's not normal."

A wave of fury washed over me. I was tired of Matt acting like Mr. Superiority.

"You guys just don't know what it's like to be in love," I said scornfully.

Talk about saying the wrong thing. Jen started to cry. I stood there, helpless. I wanted to kick myself off the bluff. Hopefully, I'd be lucky enough to land on a really sharp, pointy rock.

Matt shook his head at me, as though he didn't even have a word to describe what an idiot I was. Then he led Jen down the path. I watched the flashlight bob until it was out of sight.

Over the next few days, every time I thought of Matt with his arm around Jen, I wanted to punch a wall. Every time I thought of myself blurting out that Jen didn't know what it was like to be in love, I wanted to jump out a window.

Now I wished that my parents had taken us to Europe. Maybe I could have started a whole new life.

"I have an idea," Nicole said the following Saturday as we sat at the kitchen table, trying to decide what to do. The problem was, I didn't want to go out of the house. I didn't feel that terrific about running into Matt or Jen.

"What?" I asked listlessly.

"I should talk to Jen," Nicole said.

"What?" I blurted.

Nicole put a hand on my arm. "Just listen to me. It's the only way. I can deal with her jealousy and vindictiveness, Jonah. After all, I have you. I have to make her understand that it's just no good to keep on accusing me. She has to accept us. Then we can all be friends."

"Nicole, we can't be friends," I said.

"She lives right next door," Nicole said. "We can't go on this way. You won't sit in the backyard anymore. You won't go to the river or shopping or the movies. All you want to do is sit in the kitchen. It's the only way, Jonah."

"Nicole, it's really not a good idea," I said.

Nicole stood up. "Don't worry. Jen will understand."

Jen stared at Nicole, stony faced. She hugged her sore wrist against her chest, as though she were protecting it from Nicole.

"So you see," Nicole said in a voice as smooth and sweet as honey, "it makes sense for us to make peace. I know it must be hard. I know you still love Jonah—"

"You don't know anything," Jen said tightly.

Nicole paused delicately. "But, Jen, people break up. You have to accept it and move on. I'm a part of Jonah's life now. You're so strong and capable—"

"You don't know me," Jen said coolly. "You don't know the first thing about me. So don't tell me what I'm like."

"What I mean is," Nicole continued sweetly, "you can move on, too."

Jen eyed Nicole as though she were a specimen in biology class that she was about to dissect.

I stood there, ready to hose both girls down if necessary. I'd never felt so uncomfortable in my life.

"Thanks for the advice, Nicole," Jen said in a purr that dripped with something resembling corrosive battery acid. "I'll take it in the spirit it was given."

"May I use your bathroom?" Nicole asked, getting up.

"Why don't I just put some newspapers down for you?" Jen said, mocking Nicole's syrupy tone.

I jumped up. "I'll show you where it is, Nicole."

I led her out of the living room, to the bathroom off the kitchen.

"Whew," Nicole whispered as soon as we were out of earshot. "I'm just not getting through at all. She's really bitter."

"I really think we should go," I said.

Nicole nodded sadly. "I guess you were right, Jonah. This was a mistake. Let's give her a minute to cool off, and then say our good-byes."

"Sounds good to me," I said jumpily. I waited in the kitchen for Nicole to use the bathroom. There was no way I was about to face Jen alone. I might be stupid, but I wasn't crazy.

In a few minutes, Nicole hurried out of the bathroom. "I have an idea," she murmured to me. "Just let me see Jen alone for a minute."

"Are you sure that's a good idea?" I asked.

Nicole's hands were shoved deep in her pockets. "Trust me. I think she'll open up if you're not there."

"Just keep a large piece of furniture between the two of you," I told her. "I'll wait here."

I leaned against the kitchen counter, my foot tapping nervously. I heard the low murmur of Nicole's voice in the other room. I didn't hear a sound from Jen. That must be a good sign.

Suddenly, I heard Jen scream, "Get out of my house, now!"

I raced to the living room. Jen was standing, one arm raised toward Nicole, as if she was about to punch her lights out. Nicole jumped back behind the armchair.

"You nasty witch!" Jen screamed. "Get out! Get out! Get out!"

Nicole looked at me, shocked.

"Let's go," I said.

I took Nicole's arm and hustled her out of the room.

"Don't you *ever* come in this house again!" Jen screamed.

Nicole and I hit the porch. "I don't know what happened," Nicole said. "She went off the deep end and started screaming. Jonah, do you think she's okay?"

Mrs. Malone drove up just then. Just as she got out of the car, Jen opened the front door.

"Get off my porch!" she screamed. "Get off!"

Mrs. Malone looked shocked. None of us had ever heard Jen scream like that. Mrs. Malone started to run toward the house. "I'm sorry," I said to her as she passed us. I hustled Nicole down the porch stairs and hurried her across the lawn.

Behind us, we heard Jen burst into hysterical sobs. As soon as we reached my driveway and were out of sight, Nicole stopped.

"I think she has serious emotional problems, Jonah," she said.

"What did you say to her?"

Nicole looked mystified. "I just said that I knew how hard it was to break up with someone. How you think you'll never get over it, but someday you do. And that I hoped we could be friends someday. And she started screaming."

"Well, I guess you just pushed the wrong button," I said.

Nicole's face was intense. "You don't understand what I'm saying, Jonah. Something's wrong with Jen. Did it ever occur to you that she might have cut that rope *herself*?"

16//losing it

"Think about it," Nicole said. "It makes sense."

"It doesn't make *any* sense," I said. "Why would Jen endanger herself like that? She could have been mincemeat on those rocks."

"She'd done that swing a million times," Nicole said. "She knew she could make it. And besides, she's *unbalanced*. That's my point. It's not like she was thinking clearly."

"But why would she risk her neck like that?"

"Because she hates me, Jonah," Nicole said. "She wanted something to accuse me of. Don't you get it?"

But I was already shaking my head. "Jen is the most levelheaded person I know."

"When Jen said I didn't know her, she was wrong," Nicole said. She leaned against my car and hugged herself, her hands in her armpits. "I've gotten to know her through you. I know that she's had it rough. Her father left her. Then her brother did—first when he was a drug addict, and then when he took off for school. And she kept it all inside. That's the scary part."

"I didn't say she had a perfect life," I said. "Nicole, you're leaping to all kinds of conclusions. Jen couldn't have cut that rope. She was playing softball, remember?"

"Not the whole time," Nicole said. "She sat out two innings, remember? And she wasn't on the bleachers, Jonah. Where did she go?"

I didn't have a chance to answer. Mom called us in for Dewey's birthday lunch. Nicole waited outside to greet the giggling pint-sized horde while I helped Mom unpack the food from Rosie's Taco Kitchen, Dewey's favorite place in the world. Dewey would have tacos *and* Timmie by his side. Talk about ten-year-old heaven.

I set out the guacamole and the tacos and the beans, and I tried not to think about what Nicole was suggesting. My brain was on serious overdrive. Because I couldn't imagine Jen cracking up. She'd been through so much. How could she lose it now?

But over the next couple of weeks, Jen seemed to fall apart even more. At first Matt wouldn't tell me about her behavior, but finally, he was so freaked that he broke down and spilled his guts. I had a pretty good picture of what was going on.

Jen was nervous and jumpy at home. At work, she kept misplacing things. She claimed that she couldn't get any sleep because someone kept ringing her phone in the middle of the night and hanging up.

Then one day she claimed that Nicole tried to run her over! She said that Nicole was in a maroon car, and had driven straight toward her while she was walking to town. Jen got all scratched up when she jumped in some bushes to get away.

First of all, on the day Jen claimed Nicole was aiming a car at her, I'd been with Nicole. The entire day. And everyone knew that Nicole doesn't have a car. Mrs. Malone told my mom that Jen was probably subconsciously remembering my dad's accident. He'd thought it had been a maroon car that had driven him off the road.

Then Jen claimed that someone had left a bloody doll on her doorstep with her name written on a tag around the doll's neck. But Jen couldn't produce the doll. She said she was too scared to touch it, and when her mom went out to see it, the doll was gone.

Mrs. Malone was seriously afraid that Jen was close to hysteria.

"Poor girl," Nicole said to me sadly.

I was working on refinishing the last piece of furniture for Dad when the phone rang. It was Mrs. Malone.

Her voice sounded tight and high-pitched. "Can you come over here, Jonah? Right now?"

"Sure," I said nervously. "What is this about?"

"Just come," Mrs. Malone said, and put the phone down.

I hurried over to the Malones. I knocked, but nobody answered, so I pushed the door in and listened. I heard Jen's voice rising higher and higher.

"I'm telling you, it's not true! I wrote it for the contest! It's not *me*! Ask Jonah!"

I walked into the living room. Jen was sitting on the couch, bolt upright. Her purse was at her feet, as though she'd been about to leave when her mother stopped her.

"Here he is," Jen said with relief. It was the first time she'd been glad to see me in weeks. "Jonah, tell my mom she's crazy."

I looked at Mrs. Malone. She was holding a bunch of papers in her hand, and she sighed. "Jonah, would you read these, please?"

I took the pages and read.

"'tuesday

today, I was really flying. down below, I could see my problems—my old boyfriend, my mom ragging at me, the general utter flatline of life—but they were so far away, I didn't care.

sweet little pills. my friends . . .'"

I looked up.

"Keep reading," Mrs. Malone said grimly.

"'my friends think I'm just happy, or energetic. if they only knew about better living through chemistry!'"

I scanned the rest of the page. It was a diary. A diary of drug abuse.

"'thursday

I think I took too many today. whatever. I was wired. I needed something so bad to come down. I thought about going to Philly to score.'"

I had an awful feeling in the pit of my stomach. Was this why Jen was breaking down? And was it all my fault?

"Well?" Mrs. Malone said.

Jen looked at me eagerly. "Tell her, Jonah."

"Tell her what?" I asked, confused.

Jen's face changed. She looked angry. "Tell her that this is the essay I wrote for that contest! The Clean Teens contest!"

I held out the pages. "But Jen. This isn't . . .

it isn't the essay you wrote. I mean, I never saw it before."

Jen smacked the couch with her hand. "You know I was writing an essay!"

"I know," I said. "But this isn't it."

"That's because you fell asleep during the other version!" Jen said hotly. "You told me to make it personal, remember? Give it *zing*?"

"I guess," I said.

"So I did!" Jen cried. "This is it!"

I looked at Mrs. Malone. Her eyes were full of tears.

"Jen, we just want to help you," she said softly. "I've been through this with Scott—"

"I'm not on drugs!" Jen shouted. "It's Nicole. She did it."

Mrs. Malone slumped back in her chair. "Not this again," she whispered.

"Nicole did this," Jen said to me. "My essay was in my computer—I hadn't printed out a hard copy. She did it! She left it where she knew my mother would find it eventually."

"Where was it?" I asked.

"It was under her mattress," Mrs. Malone said sorrowfully. "I noticed it when I was changing the sheets. She must have hidden it."

"Nicole did it!" Jen cried.

"Nicole," Mrs. Malone said. "Please, honey,

be reasonable. How could Nicole do this? You've been so nervous that I've had to leave the security system on, even during the day. How could she have broken in?"

"That day she came with that phony apology and that 'let's-be-friends' bull," Jen said, her eyes lighting up. "That's when she did it!"

"But, Jen, she was with you the whole time," I said.

"She went to the bathroom!"

"But I was with her!" I said. "I waited right outside the door."

Jen's eyes filled with frustrated tears. "I don't know how she did it. But I know she did! I saw her in your backyard right after," she said to me. "She waved at me as though nothing had happened. She's trying to torture me, drive me crazy—"

"She wasn't in the yard after it happened," I said. "It was Dewey's birthday lunch that day. We didn't go out in the yard until way later."

"Do you know what she said to me that day, Jonah?" Jen asked. "Do you know why I screamed? Nicole told me that I was too square for you. That I wouldn't give you what you 'needed.' The girl is sickening!"

I was embarrassed. "Jen," I said in a quiet tone, "why would Nicole say that? It's not true.

Nicole and I haven't . . . we don't . . ."

"She hates me!" Jen shouted. "Don't you get it? She doesn't even like knowing I *exist*! She's trying to destroy me!"

"This paranoia is a symptom of your disease, honey," Mrs. Malone said. "Drug abuse is a *disease*."

Jen screamed.

Mrs. Malone got up from her chair hurriedly and went to sit by Jen on the couch.

"Honey, I know it's hard. I know you're in denial about this. But please, please be honest with me. I can help you—"

Jen stood up so abruptly, she banged her knee against the coffee table. "I've got to get out of here. You both don't believe me. Nobody believes me. She's winning!"

She started for the door, but her foot caught in her purse strap. Jen stumbled, but she didn't fall.

But her purse opened, spilling out the contents on the rug. A wallet. A candy bar. A lipstick.

A bottle of pills.

And my paring knife.

Mrs. Malone got the best help for Jen. No expense was spared.

Dr. David Marchinak is an expert in teenage drug addiction. He told Mrs. Malone that Jen's hysteria and paranoia were bad signs. But the worst was her denial that she had a drug problem.

The only solution was to remove her from her home and enroll her in a live-in drug treatment program.

17//every minute, every day

Guilt became my best friend. I greeted the monster every morning, and he hung over my bed every night like a shadow.

I thought things couldn't get much worse.

Then I got fired.

My boss told me at the end of my shift.

"Look," Andy said nervously, "don't take it personally, Jonah. I just signed on more help than I actually needed. And you were the last one in the door, so . . ."

I stared at him. He had to be kidding. The country club restaurant was always packed. I ran my feet off bussing tables and setting up. If you asked me, he needed *more* help, not less.

Andy had a funny expression on his face, like he didn't want me to argue and was afraid I'd make a stink.

"Look, I gave you two weeks' extra pay," he said. "You don't have to come in." He looked at his watch. "I've got to go. You have a good summer, Jonah."

"Thanks," I said. "You, too." But I said the words to empty air. He'd already run back to the kitchen.

I felt like a burst tire. Nicole was waiting for me at the gate, like she always was.

"What's the matter?" she asked as she slid into the front seat. "You look down."

"I just got fired," I said. I filled her in on what Andy Hollister had said.

"That's a drag," Nicole said. "But the summer is almost over, anyway." She twisted in the seat to face me. "Now we can spend every minute of every day together, Jonah! Isn't that majestic?"

"Sure," I said. Funny. A couple of months ago, if you'd asked me what my fondest wish was, I might have said spending every minute of every day with a gorgeous girl.

Now, I wasn't so sure.

Usually, I drove Nicole home to Parson's Ford at the end of the evening, leaving her on the corner of Aunt Mags's street. Then, when I got home, she wanted me to switch on my laptop once I'd brushed my teeth and was ready for bed. Nicole said she wanted to be the last person I spoke to every night. A couple of weeks ago, I'd thought that was romantic.

One night, after we'd said good night, my e-mail flag popped up. It was another e-mail message from ToddWan4, the mysterious person whose mail Nicole had inadvertently deleted.

I accessed his e-mail.

Dear JonBoy,

If this doesn't relate, sorry to bug you again. I got no response last time, but thought I'd knock on your door once again.

I'm on the trail of a girl with the e-mail address Nico91. She could have other addresses, however. If she fits the following profile, please let me know:

If you're a guy, she might have come on to you online. She might have sent a picture to you. She's blond and very beautiful. Or she could have sent music for you to download on your computer. She probably told you she was from some state in New England, like Massachusetts or New Hampshire.

She's a big MUD game player, and is a top player on PlanFam. She is also a fairly decent hacker.

If any of this rings a bell, please reply ASAP. I'll return a response w/an explanation.

Thanx.

There probably were plenty of blondes cruising the Internet. ToddWan might not be describing Nicole. But the details seemed mighty close.

I clicked on "reply" and wrote:

Dear ToddWan4,

I think I might know who you're looking for. I was contacted online, sent the picture you described, and my friend is from MA. Explanation?

I didn't want to give ToddWan any details. After all, he could be some weirdo who was stalking Nicole.

I had just finished brushing my teeth (I'd lied to Nicole about being ready for bed) when my flag popped up.

JonBoy,

I can't say for sure it's the same person. But if so, I have to issue a warning. The girl can be hazardous to your health.

E-mail isn't safe. I think we should meet, if poss.

I live in NJ. Nico tends to hone in on guys in the NE, so I'm betting you're somewhere pretty near.

Look. I don't want to sound like a crazy person or anything. But if it is the same girl, you could be in trouble. I've been looking into her family tree, and it's twisted.

I stared at the screen. ToddWan could be twisted himself. The whole thing sounded weird.

Just then, my IM—instant message—box popped up. ToddWan was looking for me. I answered with a *???*

Hey, he tapped out. *Can we meet?*

I live in Bucks County, I wrote.

Great. I'm just across the river. How about we meet in Philly? I don't have a car, but I can take the train from Trenton.

I had a sinking feeling that I was about to leave on a wild-goose chase. Or that ToddWan was a practical joker. But we fixed on a time—noon—and a place—the railroad station.

Then ToddWan's words flashed onscreen:

I don't want to freak you out. But don't tell her you're meeting me. And be sure you're not followed. Watch your back.

That sounded pretty dramatic. But was ToddWan paranoid . . . or legitimately scared?

18//the waiting room

I told my parents and an extremely pouty Nicole that I was going job hunting.

"I don't understand," she said. "Now we can spend more time together. Why do you want to get another job?"

"I just have to make the effort to look," I said. "For the sake of the parentals."

I left right after rush hour so I wouldn't get caught in traffic. All the way there, I told myself that Nicole probably wasn't Nico. And even if she was, how dangerous could a sixteen-year-old girl be? Maybe ToddWan was the excitable type.

I made good time and found a place to park near the station. It was expensive, but I didn't think I'd be too long. And at least I wouldn't have to hunt for a space.

I walked the few blocks to the station. I was still early, so I bought an orange juice and a sports magazine and settled in on one of the wide wooden benches to wait.

I checked the board. The train from Trenton was due at eleven fifty-five. ToddWan had told me that he was almost six feet tall and skinny, with sandy-colored hair. He'd be carrying a red notebook.

I read my magazine and finished my orange juice. They announced the track for the Trenton train, and I walked over to where the people would be coming up the stairs.

At eleven fifty-five exactly, people started streaming up the stairs. College kids with back-packs. Families. Businessmen and -women with briefcases, checking their watches. A woman with a stroller. No kid with sandy-colored hair and a red notebook walked up.

Irritated, I bought another magazine and another juice. The least ToddWan could do was to catch his train. But I might as well wait for the next one. I checked the board. I only had to wait another twenty-seven minutes.

The train was announced on time, on the same track as the earlier one. I waited at the top of the stairs. The same mix of passengers streamed up the stairs. And there was still no tall, sandy-haired guy.

Now I was angry. I decided to wait for one more train. I sat down again. I'd have to wait until almost two o'clock. I thought of the charges mounting in my parking garage, which was now eating up my measly savings account.

I waited through the next train. And the next. By this time, it was beginning to penetrate even my thick skull that ToddWan wasn't going to show. And that I'd better hit the road before the rush-hour traffic started at four. Or before I washed away on a tide of vitamin C.

I dumped the magazines and my juice cartons in the garbage. Disgusted, I headed for the lot to get my car out of hock. I handed over every dollar in my wallet and pointed the car toward the highway.

The first thing I'd do when I got home, I decided, was send ToddWan an e-mail that would scorch his wires. What a waste of a day! He had a nerve, trying to scare me and then not even bothering to show up! I should make him send me the money for gas and parking.

Traffic was heavy, but I finally saw the sign for the Milleridge turnoff. Then, ahead of me, I caught sight of a maroon car.

My fingers tensed on the steering wheel. A maroon car isn't that strange a sight on the highway. But this one had a black convertible top. And out-of-state plates!

I couldn't tell who was driving, or even if it

was a man or a woman. They were wearing a baseball cap pulled down low. I swung the car out into the left lane to get a better look. But I should have checked the mirror more carefully, because I cut a car off.

This guy honked at me, then kept his hand on the horn like a jerk. I had to drop back into the right lane. The maroon car suddenly pulled into the left lane. The guy—or the girl—must have really put the pedal to the medal, because suddenly, the car zoomed ahead.

I tried to get into the left lane, but now the guy with the heavy horn hand wouldn't let me in. I was boxed in!

So I lost the guy. The score for the day? Life: 2. Jonah: 0.

When I got home, Dad and Mom were fixing dinner and listening to the news. Dad was making hamburger patties, and Mom was washing lettuce for the salad. I decided not to tell them about maybe seeing the car that hit Dad. It would just stir the whole thing up again, and I didn't know anything for sure. It wasn't like I was able to read the license plate or anything.

"Nicole called," Mom said. "She's in Milleridge, shopping. She'll call back in a few minutes. You can invite her for dinner, if you want."

"Just for a change," Dad said. "Do you think she wants us to adopt her?"

"Maybe," I said.

"So, should we make another hamburger?" Mom asked.

"I guess so," I said. I stole a lettuce leaf and ate it. The newscaster started jawing about some political crisis.

Then the chirpy woman newscaster, the one with the hair that looks like a football helmet, turned to the camera.

"Tragedy struck in Trenton today, when a seventeen-year-old boy fell, or jumped, onto the tracks in front of an oncoming train. The victim was identified as Todd Waninski, a resident of Glen Willow, New Jersey. He is now in a coma at St. Teresa's Hospital in Glen Willow."

The radish I was swiping from the salad bowl flew out of my fingers and bounced across the floor.

"How many times have we told you not to play with your food?" Dad joked.

"Witnesses report seeing Waninski arguing with a boy in a baseball cap shortly before the incident. Police are asking the person to come forward with any information."

A boy in a baseball cap. A baseball cap? A *boy*?

Nicole is slender and petite. With her long hair in a cap and some kind of bulky jacket, who could tell?

A picture flashed on screen. A sandy-haired guy smiled out at me.

ToddWan.

He had warned me Nicole was trouble. Maybe he wasn't so paranoid, after all.

19//aunt mags

When Nicole called again, I lied. I told her I had some kind of stomach virus, and I couldn't pick her up. She offered to come over, anyway, and take care of me, but I managed to talk her out of it.

"You don't want to get this," I said. "It's gross."

That night, dread choked my nightmares. Every time I woke up I pictured Nicole's sweet smile, her angelic looks. I tried to imagine her slender delicate hands reaching out and pushing someone into the path of on oncoming train. . . .

And I couldn't. Nicole couldn't be Nico. She just couldn't be!

By the next morning, I knew what I had to do. I had to talk to Aunt Mags.

I told Nicole that I was still sick. She offered to come over again, but I told her that my mom had said absolutely not. I was too contagious. I whispered and coughed, then said I had to get off the phone to barf. Nicole said she'd hit the mall and buy me a present.

"Just don't buy me food," I said.

I drove to Parson's Ford. First, I drove down the block where I always left Nicole. I was looking for a maroon car with out-of-state plates, but I didn't see one.

I drove back into the center of town, parked, and found a phone booth with a phone book in it. I looked up Margaret Gemini, but there was no one by that name listed. Then I remembered Nicole had mentioned that Aunt Mags was her mother's sister. That meant that they had different last names.

Bummer!

I didn't know what else to do, so I just started driving up and down the streets of the town. Parson's Ford was smaller than Milleridge. It totally catered to tourists, and it was full of bed-and-breakfasts and restaurants and antique stores. There must have been a candle store on practically every block.

I tried dividing the town into a grid so that I wouldn't drive down the same street twice, but it was impossible. There were dead-end streets and streets that curved crazily around other streets and then doubled back on themselves. I drove and drove until I got dizzy. My stomach rumbled, and I figured it was time for lunch.

Then I saw it.

PARSON'S BED-AND-BREAKFAST
Proprietor: Maggie May Ford

Nicole had said that her aunt's name was Margaret May. It was worth a shot.

I parked the car and hurried up the stone stairs. I knocked on the door, and after only a moment it opened.

The middle-aged woman who answered looked nothing like Nicole. She had dark hair and deep brown, friendly eyes. She gave me a pleasant smile.

"Are you Maggie May Ford?" I asked.

She nodded. "Guilty. Come on in. Are you looking for a room? Are your folks with you?"

"No," I said, following her inside. "I mean, no, I'm not looking for a room, and I'm alone. I just wanted to ask you some questions, Mrs. Ford."

"Call me Maggie." She stopped in the hall. Her expression was still friendly and interested. "Well, I don't have a thing in the oven, for once. So I'm available. Shoot."

"I wanted to ask you about your niece," I said.

"My niece?" Maggie frowned.

"Nicole," I said.

"Nicole," she repeated slowly. "I don't have a niece named Nicole, young man. I have two nephews, though."

"Nicole Gemini," I said.

The smile slowly drained from the woman's face. She crossed her arms. "Nicole Gemini was a guest here. Can I inquire your name?"

"I'm Jonah Lanier," I said. "I live in Milleridge. Nicole is . . . someone I met this summer."

"I see."

"And I was hoping you could tell me . . . uh . . ." What did I want to ask, exactly? Especially since this was obviously not Nicole's aunt Mags. "Did you say she *was* a guest?"

"I asked her to leave. And I've never had to do that before, not in fifteen years of running this place."

"What did Nicole do?" I asked. Maggie hesitated, so I said, "Please. I'm trying to find out about her. She could be in trouble."

"Or causing it, more likely." Maggie gave me a shrewd look. "Oh, she had a smile that could melt butter. And she was quiet at first. Stayed in her room all day, all evening, so I couldn't even get in to clean it. She just said, 'Leave the towels by the door.'"

"When did she get here?" I asked.

"Last week in June," Maggie Ford said.

Nicole stayed in her room all the time? That didn't sound right. She had spent all of her time with me. Maybe we were talking about two different people.

"What did she look like?"

Maggie snorted. "Like an angel. Breathtaking. She started to sit in the common room, the last week or so she was here. Flirted with any man who walked into the room. Started a few fights among husbands and wives." She shook her head. "It was just plain meanness on her part. It wasn't just a pretty girl feeling her oats, if you know what I mean." She looked over at me, as though she'd forgotten I was Nicole's age.

"Well, maybe you don't. Anyway, I finally got in her room, and it was a pigsty. I read her the riot act, and she told me to mind my own business. I said, this hotel *is* my business, and I'm showing you the door. And that was that. She left in the middle of the night. Paid everything she owed, at least."

"Where did she go?"

Maggie shivered. "I don't know, and I don't want to." She tilted her head and looked at me. "You look worn out, Jonah Lanier. How about a fresh-baked muffin and some tea?"

But suddenly, I wasn't hungry anymore. "No, thanks."

"Not that it's fresh baked by me," Maggie said. "Usually, I do my own baking, but I had a kitchen fire."

I swallowed. "You had a fire?"

"Couple of days ago," Maggie said.

"Was it after Nicole left?"

"The next day, come to think of it," Maggie said. "Funny, because I was thinking, well, at least I got rid of that problem. The next thing I knew, boom."

"Boom?" I asked. My knees felt weak.

"Gas explosion," Maggie said. "What can you do? It's an old place, with old gas lines. If it's not one thing, it's another." She laughed. "Isn't that just like life?"

"Yeah," I said. "It's just like life. These days, anyway."

20//background check

In one fell swoop, I went from apprehensive to freaked. Every tiny misgiving I ever had about Nicole, every suspicion I had flattened down popped up and roared to life.

Now I didn't suspect something was wrong about my perfect girlfriend. I knew it.

Parson's Ford's town library was small, so I headed back to Milleridge. The town had raised a zillion dollars for a state-of-the-art facility.

First, I tried the Internet. I accessed the records of a major Boston paper. If Nicole was mixing fact and fiction about her background, she might really be from Massachusetts. Now what? I did a word search on "Gemini."

A bunch of things popped up, from astrology to skywatching. By the time I checked out most of them, it was almost three o'clock. I went out to the vending-machine area and bought three candy bars and ate them, one after the other, just standing there. Then I went back.

My fingers were poised over the keys, but I didn't know what to type next. I tried to remember every fact I knew about Nicole, but there weren't many. She said her parents had died coming *home* from a trip, so they probably didn't crash in Massachusetts. I typed in "small plane disasters," anyway.

It took me twenty minutes of scanning articles to come up with another big blank.

Okay. What next. I thought about the first day I'd met Nicole, when I drove her around Milleridge. She had mentioned a few things about her hometown. I strained my brain trying to remember.

"a Revolutionary War monument"

"a redbrick library"

"an inn where Washington stayed"

"a developer who wanted to knock down an old blacksmith shop"

I did a search on "shopping mall controversy" and got several articles. Two were in Boston, so I eliminated them. That left two towns, Yancy and Peasocket. I cross-checked for an inn where Washington slept, and Yancy popped up again in a restaurant review.

Then I got my big break. The *Yancy Town Crier* was on the Internet!

I accessed the paper and clicked on "search."

But search for what? I tried "Gemini" and came up empty. Apparently there were no astrology buffs in Yancy.

I drummed my fingers on the desk until the librarian gave me a nasty look.

Then my fingers seemed to move across the keys by themselves. They typed in:

"M U R D E R."

The search gave me back a long list of entries. I narrowed it down to the past five years. Then I scrolled down the titles of the articles. I started to seriously yearn for another candy bar.

I stopped at February 1991.

"Arson Investigation Reveals Murder Plot: Daughter Sought for Questioning."

I clicked on the article and a name popped out at me: Nicole Geminangi.

The fire had occurred over two weeks before the article had been written, at 7 Poplar Lane. At first, it had been ruled accidental.

The "7" in her address could have translated to gemini.7. And the fire had taken place in 1991. That accounted for Nicole's other e-mail address, Nico91.

Wilson Geminangi, 42, and his wife, Pauline, 34, had been killed. Danielle Geminangi, age 10, was hospitalized with burns, while her sister, Nicole, had also been hospitalized, in severe shock. But Nicole had walked out of the hospital one day, and the police were searching for her. It was thought she'd be close by. She'd never leave her twin.

Twin!

I'd better start from the beginning.

I found the first article, when the fire was discovered. At first, the police concluded that the twins had accidentally started the fire, playing with matches near flammable materials. There were quotes about what a great tragedy it was, and how grief had caused Nicole to stop speaking.

I clicked into the next article, and the next, as the investigation continued. At first, the police and arson investigators just started to call the fire "suspicious." Then came the "Murder Plot" article. And then came the article that explained it all.

The twins had been angry at their parents for deciding to send Danielle away to a "special school for emotionally disturbed youngsters." They had deliberately set the fire.

My whole body went cold as I read what the authorities had pieced together. The two ten-year-old girls had barricaded their parents in their second-floor bedroom. But they'd misjudged the amount of flammable liquid they needed—they'd used paint thinner—and Danielle had been badly burned.

Background stories began to surface. Reporters had asked neighbors and teachers about the "bad seed" girls.

"They were always together. And they were always a little bit strange. . . ."

"They had their own language, those two. . . ."

"Disturbed . . ."

"I called for several parent conferences. . . ."

"Cruel . . . They wrapped tape around the mouth and nose of a schoolfellow. . . ."

"Crazy . . . There was a look in her eye . . . it spooked you. . . ."

There never was a trial. The girls were too young, and the police couldn't prove it wasn't accidental. They were sent to a sanitarium for the emotionally disturbed. A grandmother footed the bills, but said she would never visit. "They killed my beautiful Pauline," she said. "There can be no forgiveness."

There were no more articles listed, so I did a word search on "Geminangi." There was just one article I hadn't seen, dated last year.

It was an obituary for Danielle.

The article briefly summarized the "incident" from five years before. A doctor was quoted, saying that "Danielle was never able to adjust to her emotional and physical scars from the incident." She was fifteen years old when she walked into the ocean one moonless night.

Her body was never found. When Nicole heard the news, she attempted suicide.

My hands were shaking, and I tucked them between my legs. Only a year before, Nicole had tried to kill herself.

Maybe, during her recovery, she had reached out to others through her computer. Maybe that's when she decided she wanted to live in the world again. Maybe she'd run away from the sanitarium, from doctors. And she'd ended up here. She wanted to belong somewhere, she'd said. She belonged with me, she'd said.

How far would she go to make sure of it?

It was getting close to dinnertime. I walked to the phones and dug into my pocket for a quarter. I dialed my home number.

"Mom? I'm at the library."

"Excuse me, Jonah. I must not have heard you. I thought you said you were at the library," Mom said merrily.

But I was in no mood to joke. "Have you heard from Nicole today?"

"She came by to see how you were doing," Mom said. "She thought you were sick, for some reason. I sent her off with Annie."

"You *what*?"

"They took their bicycles," Mom said. "I think they went to the river."

"*Alone?*" I shouted. A librarian shushed me.

"Nicole wanted to baby-sit," Mom said. "Why are you shouting? I thought you were in the library. Jonah? Jonah?"

I heard my name from a distance. Because I'd already dropped the receiver. And I ran.

21//stone cold killer

Little sisters are pests. No question. But I was fond of redheaded, recessive-gene Annie. The fact that she was in the hands of a stone-cold killer who probably now suspected that I was on to her was not good news.

I jumped into my car and peeled out of the parking lot. I drove as fast as I dared along the river, anxiously scanning the banks. I pulled over at each of my favorite overlooks. There was no sign of Annie and Nicole, and no bicycles.

I was thinking about turning around and heading for the police station when I spotted Annie's red bike. I jerked the car over and bumped along the uneven ground. Then I switched off the engine and jumped out.

I raced toward the river. I stopped with relief when I saw the sunlight glinting on Annie's red curls. She sat, her feet in the river, eating a pink ice-cream cone. Nicole was next to her.

I took a couple of deep breaths so that my

breathing was regular and even. Then I put my hands in my pockets and strolled toward them.

"Fancy meeting you here," I called. My voice came out a little shaky.

Nicole gave me a dazzling smile. It was as though she wasn't worried at all. "Hey, stranger."

I crouched down beside Annie. "How's your cone?"

"It's peppermint. Want a lick?" Pink ice cream was smeared over Annie's face. I picked up her napkin and wiped her kisser.

"No thanks," I said. "I just ate three candy bars. Any more sugar and I'll go into a coma."

Then I remembered Todd, and I winced.

"Three candy bars," Nicole said. "Are you sure you should do that, with an upset stomach?"

Oops. "I feel better," I said. "I guess it was a twenty-four-hour thing, after all."

"Lucky," Nicole said. "You never can tell with stomach disorders. You could wind up in the hospital, Jonah."

Was that a threat? I looked at Nicole, but her eyes were clear and sparkling. Her smile seemed so . . . *sincere*.

"We had fun, Jonah," Annie said to me. "Wouldn't it be fun if Nicole lived with us? I'd have a big sister. She doesn't have a family, you know. She told me. Maybe if we asked Mom and Dad, they'd let her move in."

"I don't know, Annie," I said carefully. "Nicole has grandparents who love her, you know."

"Nicole says they're mean," Annie said. "Can we ask Mom and Dad? Nicole said she'd move in if they said yes."

Nicole gave her silvery laugh. "Now, Annie, you know I didn't say that."

"Yes you did," Annie said stubbornly. She chomped down on her cone.

"Come on, squirt," I said. "Let's go home. I'll put the bikes in the trunk. And I won't tell Mom that you spoiled your appetite."

As we walked to the car, Annie skipped ahead. Nicole slipped her arm through mine.

"Annie was confused before," she said. "But wouldn't it be fantastic if I lived with your family? It would be so much fun. And we'd never have to be apart again."

"It's a nice dream," I mumbled.

"It's not a dream, Jonah," Nicole said serenely. Her grip tightened on mine. Her eyes were remote and shining, as though she were looking at something in the distance, and it pleased her. "It can be a reality. You'll see."

That night, I called the sanitarium. There was

only a recorded message, saying that it had closed. Patients had been referred to several other facilities.

I pondered my next move. I had to do something. Should I confront Nicole directly? Tell the police what I suspected?

I heard the electronic tone from my laptop that meant someone wanted to talk to me. I angled my computer over, expecting to see Nicole's name pop up. To my relief, I saw that it was AMbergrl.

Hey, Amber, I wrote. *Just the person I wanted to talk to.*

???? little ol' me? she wrote back.

I never asked you what exactly gemini.7 did to you, I wrote.

brrrrrr. bad memory. she told me to stop contacting you or she'd kill my dog.

And you took her seriously? I wrote back.

molto serioso. here's the weird part. she knew his NAME. and what kind of dog he was.

Maybe you'd mentioned it online????

don't think so. she even knew his favorite TOY. like she'd been watching the house.

I stared at the words on the screen. It was hard to believe they were true. Then again, Todd Waninski was lying in a hospital unable to breathe by himself.

That is weird, I wrote.

maybe notso. considering I knew gemini from the MUD scene.

Explain, I wrote.

nobody played PlanFam like gemini, Amber wrote. *she was fierce. took no prisoners. I mean, we all take it seriously. she took it to the death.*

How so? I prompted.

most kids set up alliances. she never did. she just set up betrayals. plus, you're not allowed to be in KILL mode on PlanFam. gemini broke the rules, then set up new rules. she took over the game. she ruled the planet.

Then what? I asked.

everybody went away. there's no PlanFam MUD anymore.

What did she do?

There was a long pause.

she blew up the planet, Amber said finally.

A chill ran through me. But Amber wasn't finished. More lines popped up on my screen.

the funny thing is, I heard some stuff. gemini made this alliance in the game with this guy online, and they agreed to meet. She ended up harassing his sister. And he says she tried to run him off the road after he broke up with her.

I tapped out, *Do you know his name?*

And I wasn't surprised when the words flashed back:

ToddWan4. we were online buds. haven't heard from him in a while.

I had to tell her. Slowly, I pecked out the story. How Todd and I had arranged to meet. That he'd been pushed in front of a train.

No words appeared for long minutes. But I waited, knowing that Amber hadn't signed off.

worse than I thought, she wrote. *so have you met this girl?*

I've met her, I wrote. *She's been here all summer. So far, she hasn't done anything to me. My family is okay and my girlfriend is in a drug rehab place. Now I think Gemini planted drugs on her. But at least jen is safe there.*

It didn't take long for Amber's words to shoot across cyber space:

don't you get it, jonah? no one is safe.

22//rescue mission

I had to be on the road by seven-thirty if I wanted to make the morning visiting hours. That night, I e-mailed Nicole, telling her that I was going river rafting with Matt the next day, all day, and then was going to sleep over. I said it was a guy thing. Matt was giving me attitude because we didn't pal around anymore.

Then I called Matt and asked him to stay out of sight for the whole day. I told him that he especially couldn't let Nicole see him. I told him not to answer the phone. If he did have to talk to her, I asked him to say I was sleeping over. I said I owed him.

"Why won't you tell me what you're up to?" he said. "And why should I do you a favor? Give me one good reason."

"Just do it for Jen," I said.

"You got it," Matt said.

I was expecting Dracula's castle, but the drug

treatment center actually looked like a nice place. It was in the mountains, and it was a rambling Swiss chalet–type building. The grounds were landscaped with trees and rosebushes and flowering shrubs.

But to Jen, it was probably a prison.

I signed in at the desk, and they made me wait in a sunny room with windows overlooking a grassy slope. I flipped through a magazine, but none of the words or pictures made sense. I tossed it aside.

A youngish man with a beard approached me.

"Jonah Lanier?"

I panicked. What if Nicole had gotten here first? "Is Jen okay?"

"Relax," the man said. "She's fine. She'll be out in a minute." He perched on the edge of a chair opposite me. "I'm her therapist, Dr. David Marchinak."

"Glad to meet you, Dr. Marchinak," I said. I eyed him warily, but he looked like a friendly bear.

"Call me David. We all use first names around here. I just wanted to brief you on how Jen is doing."

"Okay." Should I tell him now that Jen had been set up? I had thought about what to do all the way up here. From now on, it was important that I act smart. Because Nicole was a master. She would widen those blue eyes, and lie, and the lie would sound like honey. I didn't have any proof that she'd tried to run my dad off the road, or had pushed Todd in front of a train.

I had to protect Jen. She wasn't safe here. But if I told Dr. Marchinak—David—that Jen wasn't an addict, there was a good chance he wouldn't believe me. I was her boyfriend. I had every reason to lie.

"Jen is still in denial," David said. He laced his fingers together. "She has had periods of hysteria, and we've had to sedate her."

"You're giving drugs to a drug addict?" I asked. "Wise move."

David's friendly expression turned frigid. "Unfortunately, it's necessary in extreme cases. Jen had an episode this morning. She tried to run away. I just wanted to warn you that she might appear . . . listless."

My heart cracked. I had done this to Jen. My Jen. I had to get her out of here!

But I had to stay cool.

"I understand," I said, shaking my head sadly. "Poor Jen."

David nodded. "Maybe you can get through. Jen has a fixation on a new girlfriend of yours—"

"Nicole," I said. "That's all over."

"Oh?" David frowned. "When Nicole called yesterday and offered to come up for a session, I got the impression—"

An icy hand seemed to grip my heart. "Nicole called you?"

"She was very concerned about Jen," David said.

"David, Nicole and I have broken up," I said forcefully. "For good."

"Well, that might be good news. You might be able to break through to Jen." David slapped his thighs, then stood up. "Good luck."

I gave him a totally sincere, man-to-man look. "Thanks, David. And thanks for helping Jen."

He nodded. I could tell that he thought he was a lifesaving big shot instead of a pompous, clueless fraud.

He left, and a minute later, Jen came in the room. She was dressed normally, in a T-shirt and jeans, but her hair hung down without its usual curl, and her walk was more like a shuffle.

I couldn't take it. I couldn't take seeing her that way. My vision blurred, and I had to blink hard.

"Hi, Jonah." Jen eased into a chair as though her body were made of glass. "What brings you to this neck of the woods?"

It was like the old Jen, but it wasn't. Her voice was thin and watery. Her lips were chapped at the edges.

I had no time to waste. I leaned forward. I took both of her hands in mine. I expected her to pull away, but she just left them there, limp. I squeezed her hands hard.

"I believe you, Jen," I said, my voice low, but making sure she heard every word. "I know you're not on drugs. That you were never on drugs. I know that Nicole framed you."

Jen gave a little jump. She met my gaze.

"I'm sorrier than you'll ever know that I didn't believe you before. But now I do. Nicole has done this to you. And I'll be making it up to you forever. But first, I'm going to get you out of here."

At first, her pale face was a blank. My heart failed. This strange, wan Jenny was like another person. Was I too late?

Then a spark of the person I knew shone through the haze.

"Well, it's about time," Jen said. "You lunkhead." She grinned, and I knew everything would be all right.

I went back for evening visiting hours. They were more crowded. People stood around the lobby, holding baskets of fruit and stuffed teddy bears.

I signed in again, then added a second signature under my name. I spilled a glass jar full of pens on the floor so that the nurse wouldn't notice what I'd done.

I got to meet Jen in her private room. We balled up towels and made them look like a body. We covered the towels with a blanket.

I gave Jen a denim jacket and a baseball cap. She shoved her hair under it and tugged it down over her face.

And then we just walked out.

23//hiding out

It was dark when we drove out of the rehab center gates. Headlights shone behind me, family members heading back after the evening visit.

There was one problem: Which way should I turn?

I looked over at Jen. She gave me a wan smile, but I knew she was tired. It would be a long drive back to Milleridge. And by the time we got there, Jen's disappearance might have been noticed. Her mother could end up sending her right back.

We needed time, and a place to think. I couldn't believe that I hadn't planned past getting Jen out of the center.

Then, for once, life gave me a break. I actually came up with a good idea. I turned left.

"My parents think I'm spending the night at Matt's," I said. "So we're covered, as far as that goes."

"Where are you heading?" Jen asked.

"The lake," I said. "It's only about fifteen minutes from here."

"But where will we stay?" Jen asked. "The cottage is destroyed."

"The MacFarlands went to California to visit their daughter's new baby," I said. "My mom told me. Their place will be empty."

"Perfect," Jen said, closing her eyes.

I checked the rearview mirror. Most of the cars behind me had turned right, to go down the mountain. But one pair of lights stayed behind me. I speeded up, but they kept the same distance.

I looked over at Jen. Her eyes were still closed. I hoped she was asleep. I was just being paranoid about the lights. It was summer. There was plenty of traffic in the mountains.

When I turned off the main road, the lights didn't follow. Relieved, I slowed down.

There were no lights on the bumpy road leading to the cottage. The quarter moon didn't give much light, and clouds covered the stars. I drove cautiously over the ruts and bumps. Jen woke up and peered through the windshield anxiously.

I parked close to the woods, pulling the car up as far as I could so that it would be hard to see.

It was easy to break into the MacFarlands'. I knew where they kept their key: in the birdhouse perched in the tree in the backyard.

I quickly switched on the lights. Within minutes, the cottage looked cozy and welcoming.

Jen sighed and threw herself on the couch. "It's so good to be here." She looked up at me. "Thank you."

"I'll find us something to eat."

I bustled around the kitchen. I found sodas and a package of frozen macaroni and cheese. I popped it in the microwave along with a frozen chicken potpie. The MacFarlands don't believe in roughing it.

I gave Jen most of the food, and we ate every noodle and every crumb of the potpie. She put down her fork with a sigh.

"That tasted great," she said. "The food at the rehab center wasn't bad. But it tasted like sawdust."

"Jen, it was all my fault," I said. "I don't know what happened to me. Nicole took over somehow. It was like I was under a spell. I'm really sorry I hurt you. I should have believed you, not the so-called evidence."

I wanted Jen to say, *It's okay* or, *I understand*. But Jen wouldn't say that until she really meant it. I had never appreciated her honesty so much before. Even when it made me feel like a slimeball, straight up.

"She's a very clever girl," Jen said finally. She stood and picked up her plate.

I quickly rose to my feet. "I'll do the dishes," I said. "You rest."

"I think I'll take a short walk down to the lake," Jen said. "Freedom still feels good."

I washed the dishes and sponged down the counters, making it look as though no one had been there. Tomorrow morning I'd run out and buy more frozen food to replace what we'd eaten.

When Jen came back, her eyelids were drooping.

"I'm beat," she said. "I can barely keep my eyes open. I know we have things to talk about, but—"

"We'll talk in the morning," I said. "You take the bedroom. I'll sleep on the couch out here."

I wanted to kiss her good night. Just a quick kiss, on the cheek. Maybe even a short hug. Something to make me feel that even though she couldn't forgive me tonight, she would someday. But Jen knew what I wanted. She leaned over and kissed me on the cheek, her lips soft and warm.

"Good night, Jonah."

Jen disappeared into the bedroom. I got a blanket and stretched out on the couch. Crickets chirped, and I could see the fingernail moon through a gap in the curtains. Somehow, I felt more calm, more myself than I had all summer.

Soon, it would be all over. Jen and I would talk it over. We'd figure out a way to prove what Nicole had done. The two of us together could convince her mother. And then we'd tell my parents. And go to the police.

Tomorrow . . .

I wasn't sure what woke me. But when I opened my eyes, I saw flickering reflections on the wall.

The moon is really bright tonight, I thought sleepily.

But there wasn't a full moon.

I sat up. Now I could hear it—the crackle and snap of the flames. I looked out the window. The woods were ablaze. Even as I watched, sparks flew into the air, curling lazily, and headed for the cabin.

"Jen!"

I threw back the blanket and pounded to the bedroom door. I threw it open. Jen was just putting her feet on the floor.

"What is it?" she said, dazed.

"The woods are on fire," I said. "Hurry!"

We ran to the front door. I pushed, but it wouldn't open.

"Something's wedged against it from outside," I said. "There's no back door."

Jen put her shoulder against it. I did the same. The wood felt hot. We pushed. The door groaned, but didn't budge.

"The window," Jen said.

"Get our shoes," I told her. I grabbed a lamp and smashed the window. Jen hurried back with our sneakers. I shoved my bare feet into them. Then I kicked out the glass.

"Be careful," I told her. The flames were roaring now, and I could smell smoke and feel the heat on my face.

I helped Jen up on the windowsill. She balanced lightly for an instant, then jumped. I climbed up after her. I jumped onto the soft ground.

"Let's get out of here," Jen said. "Is there an alarm nearby?"

"I don't think so," I said.

"Come on. Let's get to the car."

I shook my head. "The car is too close to the woods," I said. "The gas tank might blow."

Jen's hair blew in her eyes, and she swiped at it. "Then what?"

"The lake," I said. "We can take the canoe next door to the Williamsons'. We can use their phone."

Hand in hand, we ran in the flickering light toward the lake. Suddenly, Jen stopped, pulling me up short.

"Jonah . . ." She pointed.

You would have missed seeing the maroon car in the dark. It was pulled up into the marsh grass. The light of the flames danced on the black roof. It had Massachusetts plates.

"She's here," I said. "Somewhere."

"Let's hurry," Jen urged.

We ran down the slick grass and broke through underneath the trees. Ahead of us was the slope down to the black, still lake.

A figure stood on the dock. Her white dress fluttered in the stiff breeze.

"It wasn't me!" Nicole cried.

24//cold moon

Jen and I stopped. Nicole twisted around. Her hands were firmly tied behind her back. "Do you see, Jonah?" she cried. "I didn't do it! She tied me up!"

"Who tied you up, Nicole?" I asked.

"Jen!" Nicole shouted. Her hair blew back from her face, and I could see her expression. Scared, sincere, stunned.

Every emotion she *should* be feeling, if she were telling the truth.

"Jonah, when are you going to wise up?" Nicole asked. "Jen is unbalanced; I've told you that from the beginning. How could I have tied myself up this way? Look at my ankles!"

They were tied, too. I could see the thick knots, even imagine them rubbing against Nicole's soft flesh.

"She wanted to die with you," Nicole said. "That's why she set the fire. She was willing to die herself, on that rope swing, just to get you back. Don't you see that?"

"The car," I said. "We saw your car."

"It's not mine!" Nicole said. "She rented it, maybe. I don't know! She gets day passes from the rehab center—did they tell you that? She could have left it here!"

Jen hadn't said a word.

"It's been Jen all along," Nicole said. "You've got to believe me."

"Save it," I said to Nicole. "I know the whole story about your parents."

"Okay," Nicole said. "I was going to tell you everything, Jonah. But that kind of story isn't something you launch into, right off the bat. The fire was an accident. I mean, Danielle dared me to light a fire. We were playing that we were camping. We didn't do it deliberately! Danielle was troubled, but she was my sister. I just went along with her."

Nicole began to cry. She looked so beautiful even now, standing with her hair hanging to her waist, in her white dress.

"I had a breakdown," she said. "My parents were dead, and I felt responsible. Then Danielle left me, too. But I'm not crazy, Jonah!" Nicole was begging now. "Jen is."

"Nicole—," I started.

"Wait," she said desperately. "Remember,

Jonah. Remember that you were with me every time Jen said I'd done something to her. And tonight. Were you with Jen every second?"

I remembered that Jen had walked down to the lake, and I hesitated.

"You weren't, were you," Nicole said. "I bet she went out for some air, or for a walk. That's when she lit the fire! You have to see, Jonah." Nicole's sobs echoed across the water. "I've lost everyone I've ever loved. I can't lose you, too!"

Jen still hadn't moved. Hadn't called Nicole a liar, or even looked at me.

Nicole's voice throbbed with emotion. "Please, Jonah," she whispered. She looked pale and fragile, as if she were crafted by moonlight. "Save me."

I'd been listening to her sweet voice all summer. Everything she said had the ring of truth. And how could Nicole have tied herself up that way? But for the first time, I didn't listen to the words. I listened to my heart. Because I'd learned something important: What was love, if you didn't believe in the person you cared for?

I took Jen's hand firmly. "No, Nicole. I can't save you. I don't think anybody can."

Nicole let out a scream of anguish. Then she jumped off the dock into the dark lake.

25//black water

"She can't swim," I said.

Jen and I slid and slipped down the slick grass to the shoreline. Nicole didn't surface.

"Her legs are tied," I said. "I have to dive in, Jen."

"Don't, Jonah," Jen begged. "It's a trick. I just know it. She's down there, underwater, waiting for you."

"I can't let her drown," I said, kicking off my sneakers.

I felt the shock of the cold water as I waded into the lake. I swam out to where Nicole had dropped off the dock. Then I ducked underneath the water.

Under the surface, it was pitch dark and eerie. I swam carefully along the dock. Maybe Nicole had gotten caught on the pilings somehow, or her foot had caught in some weeds.

Then, ahead of me, I caught sight of a faint

gleam. Something white waved ahead of me. Nicole's dress.

With a final kick, I reached out and grabbed the material. I pulled, and the filmy material floated toward me, weightless.

My lungs were bursting. I surfaced, gulping air. I held the white material aloft.

"Jen! I found—"

But there were two figures on the shoreline now. Nicole stood next to Jen. She was wearing a white sleeveless top and long skirt, and I realized I was holding her gauzy shirt.

A faint shaft of moonlight glittered on something shiny. A knife blade. As I watched, Nicole lifted it to Jen's throat.

"It's time to end this, Jonah," she said.

I felt paralyzed with terror. But somehow, I was moving toward shore. "Nicole, let's talk."

"Now you'll talk. But you won't listen," Nicole said wildly. "You still think that Jen is perfect. You won't admit she's bad."

"I'm listening, Nicole." I pushed against the water. It felt so heavy. I'd never reach Jen in time.

"I had to get your attention," Nicole said petulantly. "You have to listen, Jonah! You must love me. You just tried to save me. That proves it."

I saw Jen swallow. Her eyes were wide and stayed on the knife blade.

Nicole had lied to me all summer. Now, it was my turn.

"I do love you, Nicole," I said. "I realized it when you jumped off the dock."

The knife pressed against Jen's throat. "Don't make me mad, Jonah," Nicole said. "You're trying to trick me."

"No, I swear it's true!" I hit the shoreline, close to her now. I could see the fear in Jen's eyes clearly.

Nicole backed up, holding Jen next to her, taking backward steps up the slope. I followed, taking baby steps, not wanting to scare her.

"I'd do anything for you, Jonah," Nicole said. "Don't you see that? I had nothing before you."

"I know," I said. "You were lonely."

"I was!" Tears glittered in Nicole's eyes. "No one realizes that. I needed you."

She backed up the hill, and I kept coming.

"I'm here," I said. "You're not alone."

We stood a few paces from each other. Nicole looked down at me from her position slightly above me.

I remembered Amber telling me how fiercely Nicole had fought for a family in the MUD game. Quickly, I said, "My parents want you to live with us. They know you're alone. And they love you, too."

Nicole's face softened. "They do? They really love me?" She lowered the knife slightly.

I took a baby step closer. "Would I lie to you?" I said. "And I'm sensing something. Could it be . . ."

Jen tensed. Nicole looked at me, puzzled.

"Nerd alert!" I yelled. At the same instant, I threw the wet shirt. Jen was already bending her knees and pulling away.

The wet shirt fell over Nicole's head. It clung to her face, and she grabbed for it, off balance on the wet grass.

Jen shot out a leg, tangling it between Nicole's ankles, and Nicole went down. She slid down the slope and lay still at the bottom.

"Jonah?" Jen whispered.

I ran down the hill and stopped a few feet away from Nicole. She lay curled on her side, her face toward the water. A rapidly spreading red stain dampened her white tank top.

She'd fallen on her knife.

"We'd better call an ambulance," I said.

Jen nodded. "And the police," she said.

But already, we could hear the sirens.

26//safe haven

They took her away in the ambulance. There was no siren. There wasn't any need for hurry. Nicole was dead.

We talked to the police separately. It seemed to take hours. Finally, when Jen fell asleep on a policewoman's shoulder, they told us we could go. They'd need us for more statements in the morning.

The firemen were still hosing down the woods, and the police were still looking in the shallow waters of the lake for the knife when they drove us away.

Because it was so late, and it would be hours before my parents could get there, the police brought us to a motel. They got us two rooms side by side and told us to get some sleep. Our parents should reach us by dawn.

"Sleep?" Jen rubbed her arms. "I don't think I'll ever sleep again."

We went into our separate rooms. I turned on

every single light and the TV. Then I sat on the bed. Jen was right. I couldn't sleep.

I heard a soft knock on the connecting door. I opened it. Jen smiled weakly at me.

"I'm afraid to be alone," she said. "And I smell like smoke. I really need a bath, but I'm afraid to be in the bathroom alone. Isn't that stupid?"

"Not if you were just almost killed," I said.

"It all feels so unbelievable," Jen said. "Hey, let's take a swim in the pool. It's a warm night. And I want to get the smell of this whole experience off me."

We grabbed towels and headed for the pool. It was closed, of course, but we climbed over the fence easily. The lights were out, and the water lapped at the concrete edge, dark and still.

Jen slipped out of her jeans, but kept her long T-shirt on. I sat on the edge of the pool in my boxers while she eased into the water with a shiver.

She ducked underwater and came up laughing.

"It feels great," she said. "Come on in."

I slipped into the cool, dark water. She was right. It felt great. The chlorine would wash away the smell of smoke.

I paddled over to her and slipped my arms

around her. We hung suspended in the water, cold skin against cold skin.

"You were so brave," Jen whispered.

"You were the one with a knife at your neck," I said.

We kicked our legs gently, keeping ourselves afloat.

"She really tried to get you on her side," Jen said. "You could have believed her. You could have thought it was me who was crazy."

My arms tightened around her. "I'll never not believe in you again, Jen. You're the sanest person around. I know you. And I *still* love you," I said teasingly.

She giggled softly. "It feels good to have you tease me again."

We bobbed in the water like seals. Jen's arms felt so good around me.

"Do you forgive me, then?" I said.

"I guess I have to," Jen said. "You saved my life."

Keeping one arm around each other, we swam together slowly, lazily, toward the shallow end of the pool. Our feet drifted down and touched bottom.

"It's finally over," Jen said. "I thought it would never—"

Suddenly, she stiffened. "Jonah," she whispered. Her voice shook with fear.

"What is it?"

"Over there," she whispered. "There's something—someone—on the bottom of the pool."

"There can't be," I said. My eyes strained through the darkness. "Maybe it's a towel . . ."

But the dark patch moved suddenly, with a great lurch, and she burst above the surface, screaming, her blond hair wet and lank and twisted down her back.

Nicole. Rising in the air, the knife lifted, ready to fall on us.

27//gemini

I pushed Jen away as hard as I could, and leaped the other way. As I smashed into the side of the pool, I felt a sting on my ankle. I turned, the splash of the water blinding me.

Nicole was going after Jen.

I saw only one way to stop her. I catapulted out of the pool. Balancing on the rim, I leaped off, right on Nicole.

She collapsed underneath me, underwater. I put my fingers around her neck and squeezed. She thrashed, and I lost my grip. She shot upward toward the surface, and I caught her ankle. She twisted away, and her head hit the side of the pool with a *crack*.

She slumped, falling underwater. I got my hands underneath her armpits and dragged her to the steps of the pool. I hauled her out, gasping.

"Jen, call the police. Get the motel guy. Hurry."

"I won't leave you alone with her," Jen said, shaking.

"Get me something to tie her with, then."

Jen ran to the lifesaving equipment. She brought me a rope, and together, we tied Nicole up.

"Jonah, she was dead," Jen said. "We saw her. How—"

I was busy binding Nicole's wrists. I stopped and picked up her arm. I held it in the faint light. I could just make out the scars on her hands.

"I don't think this is Nicole," I said.

Danielle awoke when the police and ambulance arrived. The paramedics checked her vital signs, and she was fine. One bandaged her head while another tortured me with disinfectant for the knife wound on my ankle.

Danielle looked at me. It was eerie how identical she was to Nicole. "Jonah, help me," she said. "They'll take me away again. They'll take me away from Nicole."

Tears rolled down Danielle's cheeks. It was amazing. She was Nicole's exact double.

"Nicole's gone," she said. "I saw them take her away. Where did they take her?"

"To the hospital," I said.

"It's not right to divide two sisters," Danielle

said. "Talk about family values. Doesn't anyone care? I *am* Nicole. And she's me. They tried to split us up. It was so unfair."

Jen shivered and moved close to me. She didn't take her eyes off Danielle.

"Get away from him," Danielle snapped. "I took care of you that day at the river. You were supposed to hit those rocks! Then Nicole showed up. She didn't know I was with you, Jonah. Just like that day at the restaurant. I thought it was time Jen saw me. Nicole always took things too slowly. She's a wimp sometimes. That's why she needs me! She tried to get away. She thought you could take her away."

"The gloves," I said. "Every time Nicole was wearing gloves, it was you."

Danielle beamed at me. "My idea. And didn't you like me better, Jonah? Admit it."

Jen and I stared at her, horrified. Her grin looked like a death mask. The bandage on her head was stained with red.

"Did you print out my diary?" Jen asked.

"Nicole did," Danielle said. "She's the cyber geek. She left the bathroom window open, and I crawled in. I decided to pump up the volume and get you really angry. While you were screaming, Nicole was breaking into your files. Talk about wimps!" Danielle mimed a scream.

"*Aaaah. Aaaah.* What an easy target you were, Jen."

I slipped my hand into Jen's. Danielle's head swiveled like a mechanical doll's. "Jonah, we both loved you. We loved you so much."

I stared at her in horror.

"And now we all can be together," she said. "Nicole wanted you for herself. She didn't think it could work, all three of us. But it can."

The paramedics gently lifted her and placed her on the stretcher.

"Where am I going?" Danielle asked, twisting around one way and then the other. "Where are you taking me? Don't take me away from Jonah!"

They wheeled her toward the ambulance.

Danielle sat bolt upright, startling Jen and me. We jumped back.

She screamed at the top of her lungs. Her voice echoed across the parking lot and seemed to ring from the tops of the mountains themselves. It was like an animal's cry, full of pain and abandonment.

"Nicole! Nicole! Help me! Don't leave me! Nicole!"

epilogue

Summer was over. The torture commonly known as high school would begin in only three days.

At least I'd had a blast for the last weeks of summer. I hadn't done much of anything, but I'd done everything with Jen. We had even perfected the art of bicycle riding while holding hands.

And they say I have no talent!

I hadn't visited the chat room in weeks. I'd given Amber an update, and I'd started an e-mail correspondence with Todd Waninski while he was still in the hospital. He'd recovered completely from his accident, and he'd be starting school on time. On crutches, but on time.

But I didn't hang out in chat rooms anymore. Then, one rainy night, I clicked on to check it out.

A funny girl named KCRyder was discussing the chances of the Yankees being in the World Series. I made a few snappy comebacks, and she asked for my stats. After I gave them to her, she said:

16/f. want to head for a private room, JonBoy?

I smiled.

Sorry, I wrote. No *can do. I've got a steady girl.*

So wut? KCRyder wrote back. *I've got a boyfriend. What harm can it do?*

I laughed.

You'd be surprised, I tapped out.

A hand snaked out from behind my shoulder. Jen laughed as she shut off my computer.

She slipped her arms around my neck from behind.

"You said it, buster. No more cyber dream girls for you."

I leaned against her. I felt her heart beat against my back.

"From now on, this is reality central," I said. "Because my dream girl is right next door."

A **SNEAK PREVIEW** OF THE NEXT
SUSPENSE-FILLED RIDE DOWN THE
INFORMATION SUPERHIGHWAY!

---

danger.com

@2//Firestorm/

by

jordan.cray

11//jitters

It was surprisingly easy to sneak out of my house. My parents are both early-to-bed people. Even on Friday nights, they usually hit the hay around ten o'clock and fall asleep reading in bed. They aren't exactly party animals.

Maya didn't have a problem, either. Her bedroom is on the first floor, so she just climbed out her window.

It was a long bike ride out over the railroad tracks to the north part of town. Out there are a bunch of seedy-looking houses and big warehouse buildings that look totally spooky at night. I was actually relieved to see the lights of the Beachway Diner.

The place had that American grease-pit quality from the outside. It was one of those old diners from the early sixties, I guess. Someone had tried to spruce it up with pink paint on the trim. They must have gotten a deal on the paint, because it was the ugliest shade of pink you ever saw. I could just see them walking into Home Depot and asking for "something in the Pepto-Bismol range." Which is not a product an eating establishment would want to bring to mind, if you ask me.

We cycled past the diner, then locked our bikes to a sign a couple of blocks away.

"Okay," I said. "Let's go over the plan one more time. You go in first. You sit at the counter all the way to the left. Then you check out the place and make sure that you don't recognize anyone. If you do, you get coffee to go and split right away. I wait here for five minutes. Then I come in and go to the last booth on the right. You watch the street. When you see someone familiar, you give me the high sign, and I walk out."

Maya nodded. "Hopefully, he or she won't recognize you."

"Right. Or you," I said.

We both had baseball caps on. Maya had tucked her hair up inside it and pulled the brim way down over her forehead. In the cap and her denim jacket and jeans, Maya looked like a boy. We were counting on the fact that 60.MAN, whoever he or she was, wouldn't recognize her. Maya was so engulfed in denim that *I* could barely recognize her.

"You slip out when you can," I said. "And we meet back here. It's a foolproof plan, right?"

"Check," Maya said. "You scared?"

"Nah," I said.

"Me, too," Maya said. She grinned.

I pulled down the brim of her cap a little more. "Get going," I said. "And be careful, will you?"

Maya nodded. I watched her head down the block and walk slowly up the stairs to the entrance. The the door *swooshed* behind her.

I waited five minutes. Each minute felt like an hour. Then I followed her inside.

The bright lights made me blink for a minute. At least on the inside the place looked clean and almost cheerful. The upholstery was cracked and old, but the chrome shone and colorful signs advertising specials were hung over the grill. The place was deserted, except for a beefy guy drinking coffee and reading a newspaper. Maya sat on a stool at the very end of the counter, close to the side door.

I hesitated for a minute. When 60.MAN had told me to sit in the last booth on my right, did he mean on the right from the front door, or from the side door? Most people came through the side door, since that's where the parking lot was.

I wished I could consult with Maya, but she was ordering tea from the only waitress. So I just turned to my right and walked all the way to the end of the row of booths.

I ordered coffee from the waitress. I didn't really like coffee, but it seemed like the thing to do.

I looked at the menu, but I wasn't hungry. The thought of a cheeseburger just wasn't too tempting when I was waiting for a mad bomber. On the left side of the menu there were all these Asian specialties, like spring rolls and shrimp with basil and mee krob, whatever that was.

I hunched over my coffee. I kept glancing out into the dark street. When I got tired of that, I watched the clock over the grill. The waitress refilled my cup.

The clock hands kept turning. Eleven-fifty. Eleven-fifty-five. Straight up, twelve o'clock midnight. Five after twelve. And nobody showed up. I was starting to have severe caffeine jitters.

Suddenly, at about 12:10, customers started to pour in. It started out as a trickle and turned into a stream. Some of them sat at the counter, and some groups went into booths. They all asked for tea and ordered without looking at the menu, as though they came here all the time.

And they were all Asian.

I overheard the group in the next booth, talking about work, and I realized that they all must be factory workers. They'd just gotten off their shift.

The graveyard shift. Just like 60.MAN had said.

I took a sip of my coffee. It was cold. My stomach was clenched in about a million knots. Something was weird. Something was wrong. I looked over at Maya, and she lifted one shoulder in a shrug. She didn't know what to do, either.

My hands were shaking, and I put them in my lap. There was a long tear in the upholstery next to my leg. I guessed it was expensive to fix something like that. Somebody had covered it with duct tape, and I started picking at it nervously.

I was so jittery, I didn't realize that I'd unfastened half the tape until it was too late. I quickly started to smooth it down before the waitress came back over. But she was too busy filling orders right then.

That's when I noticed that the tear went all the way down to the floor. And it was a straight tear, as though someone had split the upholstery with a penknife. Weird.

I heard the chatter of a language I didn't understand. And the same words kept drumming in my head, over and over.

The graveyard shift. The graveyard shift.

I leaned down, disappearing below the table, to peel off the rest of the tape.

I bent the vinyl upholstery back.

Underneath the seat of the booth was a hollow space. Resting on the floor, I could clearly see a small canvas tote bag.

Now who, I wondered, would rip open the upholstery of a booth in order to secrete their bag underneath the seat?

I didn't have to ask the question. The answer had danced along my nerves and jump-started my heart.

Someone planting a bomb.

Was it possible? Was I caught in a trap?

The Asian voices pounded in my ears. I couldn't understand what they were saying, but I imagined them saying "graveyard, graveyard" over and over.

I came back up, slamming my head on the bottom of the table. I didn't even feel it. I fell out of the booth and shot to my feet.

"Everybody out!" I shouted. "Move fast!"

Nobody moved. Maya looked at me, her eyes wide.

"It's a bomb!" I said. "Just move!"